To Maria

Queen of the library desk. Hope you enjoy it!

Lots of love,

Ned

# About the Author

Noel Duffy was born in Dublin in 1971 and studied Experimental Physics at Trinity College, Dublin, before turning his hand to writing. He co-edited (with Theo Dorgan) *Watching the River Flow: A Century in Irish Poetry* (Poetry Ireland, 1999) and was the winner in 2003 of the START Chapbook Prize for Poetry for his collection, *The Silence After*. His work has appeared widely in Ireland, as well as in the UK, the US, Belgium and South Africa. More recently he was the winner of the Firewords Poetry Award and has been a recipient of an Arts Council of Ireland Bursary for Literature.

Noel holds an MA in Writing from the National University of Ireland, Galway, and has taught creative writing there and at the Irish Writers' Centre, Dublin, and scriptwriting at the Dublin Business School, Film and Media Department. He currently lives in Dublin where he writes for film and television.

# The Return Journey

# and

# Our Friends Electric

Two Novellas

Noel Duffy

Ward Wood Publishing
www.wardwoodpublishing.co.uk

Published by Ward Wood Publishing
6 The Drive
Golders Green
London NW11 9SR
www.wardwoodpublishing.co.uk

The right of Noel Duffy to be identified as author of this work has been asserted by him in accordance with the Copyright, Designs and Patent Act, 1988.
Copyright © 2011 Noel Duffy
ISBN: 978-0-9566602-5-1
British Library Cataloguing in Publication Data. A CIP record for this book can be obtained from the British Library.

Designed and typeset in Garamond
by Ward Wood Publishing.
Cover Images: Businessman Thinking by Konradbak, Agency Dreamstime; The Samuel Beckett Bridge by Lokono, Agency Dreamstime; Young Man Singing by Jacekkadaj, Agency Dreamstime.
Cover design by Mike Fortune-Wood.
Printed and bound in Great Britain by
MPG Biddles Ltd, King's Lynn, Norfolk.

# Contents

# The Return Journey

I hadn't expected it to be so cold – even in April. For some reason, I remembered that Ireland was surrounded by the Gulf Stream, which accounted largely for its moderate climate. A strange thought to have, standing with the Atlantic Ocean up to my chest. Strange to have any thoughts at all under the circumstances. My jeans stuck to my legs like iron casts. I could sense the blood running from my calves, my toes already growing numb in my hiking boots. I could hardly breathe.

Did I intend to keep walking? I wasn't sure anymore. This was one thing I can say for certain that I hadn't reflected upon. I just found myself in the sea. It was only when I felt that sharp shock of the cold water, like a brace tightening about my body, that I realised it was a moment of choice. *The* moment of choice you could say: to walk backwards to the shore, or forwards into the grey, heaving mass of the ocean.

\*

I worked for the life insurance division of a respected bank in Zurich. I had taken up my position two days after receiving my degree in Business and Economics from the University of Bern. It was a good job with a good salary. I cannot say I was happy, but since I did not know what happiness was, I hadn't realised I was unhappy yet. In university I had few friends. I went to lectures and left afterwards. I bought all the textbooks so that I would not have to go to the library. I sat my exams. I passed my exams. If anyone from my class had bumped into me on the street or in a café, I doubt that they could even have recalled my name. I most certainly wouldn't have remembered theirs.

In any case, happiness wasn't my goal in life. I came to think of people as essentially unpredictable and unreliable. And what, in the end, had we to say to each other? *Where do you work now? Oh, very good. Are you married? Oh, that must be wonderful. Any children?*

I'm not saying this wasn't difficult for me. All those awkward moments when I couldn't find the correct words appropriate to a situation. It was difficult certainly. Sometimes I felt as though the trick to life – if it could be found – was to learn, somehow, to breathe under water.

In the bank I was finally in my element. I did my job and took some pleasure from it. I was efficient and well respected. At least I had thought so every time I received a small increase in my salary and a step up to the next grade. I should point out there were many and I was a great distance from the top. But then, I was no longer at the bottom either. At the end of every day my in-tray was empty, and I took some satisfaction in that achievement. My accounts always balanced, and I'd been trusted with relatively important customers within six months of starting. After four years, my workload and responsibilities had increased incrementally and, at times, so had the pressure.

One Friday afternoon, just after lunch, the lumbering form of my supervisor François approached my desk. (He preferred me to use the term *boss* but I never did.) This was unusual. François was a man who only left his desk if he needed to use the bathroom or attend a meeting with his boss, Silka. (He preferred the term line-manager.) Rather than make the short walk to my office, if something needed to be discussed, he would phone me and summon me to his slightly bigger office – no matter how trivial the issue.

'Hermann, we appear to have a problem,' he said gravely, as he stood by my desk. He made every minor matter into a grave problem.

'Yes?' I replied absently.

'Yes.'

He paused for effect, and looked at me like a disappointed father – a role he most certainly did not fulfil in my case, or in anyone else's for that matter.

'It's the Herr Dessinger account.'

'Yes... I have dealt with the matter. Some weeks ago I believe. Let me check my – '

'Well, yes. That's the problem. You have dealt with the matter. It is, in fact, a very serious issue – and a very difficult and sensitive one for the bank. I should say, for me also – given that you are under my supervision.'

'In what way serious?' I asked, beginning to believe him for once.

Although the office was occupied only by me (this had been part of my most recent change of status) he leaned down close, as though he was afraid we might be overheard.

'You have paid the wrong dividend.' He said it in French.

'Oh!' I said, taken aback. This was indeed serious. 'Well, we can pay the surplus in some way. Without making our error apparent. There must be some procedural... Has it become legal yet?'

'No. There is no surplus to be actuated,' he said in a whisper. 'You have *overpaid* on the policy by a significant figure. I will need, of course, to call a meeting immediately with Frau Libnovsky.'

The way he referred to Silka as 'Frau Libnovsky' in my company irked me. And what irritated me further was that he insisted I do likewise. Even Frau Libnovsky herself felt uncomfortable with François's somewhat outmoded formality.

He then placed a page on my desk as though it were my final notice.

I looked down slowly at the document. I studied the figures for a moment, my eyes drawn down to a number highlighted in green. (Another of François's vanities was to use all possible office stationery.) It was very serious indeed. The amount was slightly greater than three times my salary for the current year.

François hovered above me for a moment, walked to the door, then turned.

'The meeting with Frau Libnovsky will take place in the conference room on Monday at 2pm sharp. I'll see what I can do for you,' he added, as though he meant it.

He disappeared. I looked down at the page again. This was bad, very bad. To underpay a policy was an embarrassment for the department, but to overpay was a direct loss for the bank. One simply couldn't ask a customer (particularly a recipient of a policy such as Frau Dessinger) to repay part of their dividend. She was, one would imagine, still in mourning for the death of her husband, though this was not generally considered to be the case inside the office. In short, it would reflect very poorly on us and, with a customer of this kind, it was simply not even considered. To add insult to injury, I could see that François was immensely satisfied by my error.

I hardly slept that night or the following one. On Sunday, I stayed in my apartment when it was my habit to go the café for lunch and read the weekend papers. I couldn't understand how I had made such a mistake, particularly with an account of such importance. The claim had been processed some months back, and I was struggling to remember the specific decisions made regarding the matter. It had been a very busy period. Even so, I had been careless. And, worse still, my carelessness had been noted.

On Monday morning, I lay in bed staring at the wall, more tired than I had been when I went to sleep the night before. The exhaustion had accumulated with each agitated night's sleep, and by now I could hardly think straight. I struggled to the bathroom. I studied my face in the small, oval mirror and noticed that the tiredness showed. I knew François would notice it also. I had not shaved all weekend and a thick, black stubble had formed about my jaw. I filled the washbasin with warm water and applied shaving foam to my face.

And just then, perhaps because of my fatigue, I had a moment of clarity. I *had* given Frau Dessinger the correct payment. François had calculated the figure using the guidelines for the previous financial quarter. Herr Dessinger's claim had matured (a beautiful euphemism I thought) on the first day of the current quarter. Yes. I remembered now. The technocrats in the central bank had introduced an index-related incentive for life insurance policies in an attempt to encourage first time employees to enter the market – which was partly why it had been so busy that week. In their haste they had neglected to specify that this change should apply only to new customers and, as a result, the people most likely to benefit were the clients with large policies. Clients such as Herr Dessinger. Or, should I say, his wife. (It is one of the great ironies of life insurance that the person who holds the policy is the only person never to benefit from it directly.) How could I have not remembered earlier? François had thrown me off balance. A smile formed on my lips, made slightly ridiculous by the white of the shaving foam.

He was wrong. I was right.

It was a strange sensation. I can only call it a sense of triumph, though I thought at that moment it was the same as happiness. I looked forward to catching his eye in the lobby, or in the lift, or as I passed the open door of his office. I would say nothing. I would let François call me to the meeting scheduled with Silka to discuss the matter that afternoon. I would point out his error there.

It couldn't be better. François spent all his time trying to impress Silka, though she would clearly never find a man such as François attractive. (Or me for that matter, but I, at least, had the intelligence to recognise the fact.) Yes, it was perfect. I would even use a green highlighter pen to draw attention to the calculation in question. When he looked in the mirror as he shaved that slightly puffy face of his the following morning, he too would see tiredness in his eyes. I was feeling immensely giddy at the prospect.

*

I arrived at the hostel on the Dingle Peninsula weighed down by my large rucksack. The building was a big renovated farmhouse, hidden from the road by a line of oak and hazel trees. The rounded crests of the MacGillycuddy Reeks hovered above its slated roof, hazy like a painted backdrop. Daffodils gathered in clumps along the gravel path that led from the gate. By the door, a black cat snoozed in the sunlight, glanced up for a moment as I approached, then closed its eyes again.

As I took off my rucksack in the lobby, a middle-aged woman in a floral dress and red batik scarf came from an office behind the counter.

'I would like a room. Single if possible,' I said.

'Yes. This is not a problem. Ve have many rooms available at this time,' she replied with – I guessed – a

Bavarian accent and broad smile. I was caught off guard. I hadn't expected or wanted to meet any Germans. 'For how many nights you vill be staying?'

I was flustered for a moment, then replied as coldly as possible to discourage any further conversation, 'One.'

I picked up my rucksack and walked down the corridor to the left, which was lined with doors.

She called out after me, 'Sorry... Sorry, sir.'

I turned.

'Vot is your name?'

'Peter,' I replied, 'Peter Kostik,' and wondered if she would get the subtext.

'Peter. Take any room except sree. Ve have an Australian girl, Suzanna, in this room. She is very nice. Perhaps you could – '

'Thank you,' I said, then continued down the corridor without looking back.

'It's eleven euros per night. Fifteen with breakfist,' she called after me again. 'Do you vant breakfist in the morning?'

This time I didn't respond but walked towards the room furthest from the office, and that Australian girl whose name I had already forgotten.

\*

The meeting with François and Silka was to take place after lunch. I had gone to eat in a restaurant I only went to on special occasions. It was overpriced, given the quality of the food, but I liked the fact that you could eat in privacy in a booth.

For a change I sat in the window seat, but I hadn't really noticed the view. I was too busy rehearsing the exact manner with which I would humiliate Herr Supervisor.

17

Should I let him say his piece about the damage to the reputation of the bank? The loss of goodwill? The matter of expense that would have to be addressed? But I shouldn't let it go too far or Silka might see that I was beginning to behave in a manner as petty as her admirer. Yes. Let him walk the plank. But only seven feet. One way or the other, by the end of the meeting, he would be in the water.

As I drank my coffee, I noticed a young couple that had stopped in front of the restaurant window. They leaned close to each other and spoke, then she brought her hand up to his face and touched it, before kissing him. I wondered how it would feel. For someone to reach out like that and touch your face. I watched her long fingers as they traced a pattern on his cheek. She was about to kiss him again when she noticed me staring at her. She glanced at me for a moment, then kissed him anyway. I finished the last dregs from my cup as the couple walked away hand in hand. I left an unusually large tip discretely beneath the saucer, then put on my overcoat and left.

I cannot say why it happened. Perhaps it was the lightness I felt after the stress of the weekend. And the sense of release also. I was walking across the park, as I had done each morning and evening going to, and returning from, work. And that day, also, as I walked back to work from the restaurant.

It was a nice park. I suppose you could even say it was pretty. I liked it. It was relaxing before and after the pressure of a day in the office. A small river cut through its centre lined by sycamores, and there were benches about the fountain where people often sat to eat lunch on warmer days. Today, it was cold with heavy rain clouds gathered in the sky above. There were few people to be seen.

Given my mood, I would say that at the time I hardly noticed any of this. The trees, the river, the fountain, the people. They were just there. As I walked across the small bridge over the river, my shoelace came undone and I bent down to tie it. I had only bought these shoes a couple of weeks before and the nylon of the laces was prone to loosening. On another occasion this would have irritated me. But today, it didn't matter. I tied the lace without thinking.

As I stood up I felt suddenly light-headed. I regained my balance and looked straight up just as the sun broke through the leaden clouds. I shall not try to describe more than that. If I were a poet I could find the form of words to tell you why these clouds, on this particular day, seemed so fantastically different than they had on any day before, or any day since. Strange that they had always been there and I had never looked up and noticed.

I stood there staring for what must have been a couple of minutes though I can say, for that time, I was totally unaware of time. Someone walking by may have thought I had lost my mind, and in a sense they might have been correct.

And then I became aware of myself again, self-conscious as I stood beneath the sky that I hadn't noticed before. I wasn't sure what had just happened. It felt like...Well, it felt like happiness I suppose. Real happiness. My God, how long had it been since I had known that feeling.

I sat down on one of the benches by the fountain. I had to gather my thoughts. Quite suddenly, I felt very afraid, not because I had become aware of something terrible (though in a way I had) but because I had become aware of something beautiful. I mean this in a way I had never used the word before. Not pleasant. Not pleasurable to the eye. Not nice. But profoundly beautiful – in the sense, I imagined, the word was meant when it was first spoken as someone searched their memory and found that there was no term to describe what they had felt and made one up. Beauty. Full.

At that moment, sitting there on a damp bench, I knew that it wasn't just François who was wrong. I was wrong. The people walking by in the park were wrong. We were all wrong. And everything we stood for: wrong. How could we not notice? How could we go on every minute of every day and not notice such things? I realised I knew absolutely nothing and that is why I was so afraid. And it was a fear that I knew I couldn't turn away from. I must face it, understand it, tease it out.

I should have felt sorry for us all, that we had become so blinded, but I felt nothing for these people walking by, going back to their offices for meetings with clients, or to write cheques to bank officials or tax collectors, or letters to people like me. I felt as if I were floating above it all: above the people, above the buildings and streets, above the very city itself; as though, for a moment, gravity had lost its hold on me and I was beyond its reach.

By the time I got to the Life Insurance Division office I was late for the meeting. I could see the smug satisfaction on François's face as I blustered into the room. I didn't even take off my coat.

'Ah, Hermann, we have been waiting for you,' he said, glancing from me to Silka. 'You are late.'

I threw my briefcase onto the table, pulled out the file for Herr Dessinger's account, and opened it to the page with the relevant paragraph highlighted with that green marker-pen.

'Third paragraph. Calculation made as per current financial quarter. Central Bank Directive 376a, paragraph

3,' I said matter-of-factly. 'The dividend paid on the policy was correct.'

I took no satisfaction in the act. It simply didn't matter .

François looked at my notes, dumbstruck. 'I see,' he mumbled to himself as I walked towards the door. Silka looked on in bemusement, which only hours before I would have relished. Now it was irrelevant.

The next day I resigned from my position and bought a one-way ticket to Ireland. François was furious. For the second time in a week he had come to my office.

'You're in breach of contract,' he fumed, standing there with a large folder under his arm. 'You can't leave without – '

'I don't care,' I said, taking a silver pen from the desk-drawer that my father had given me when I graduated.

'I will make sure that you will not receive any salary for the months of February, March and April unless you give the department at least – '

'I don't need the money,' I said. I brushed past him, his mouth open and quivering with rage, then turned in the doorway: 'What would I spend it on anyway? Better life insurance?'

\*

I should have been relieved that the hostel was almost empty, but I wasn't. From experience I have discovered that it is often easier to remain anonymous in a crowded room than in one with only one or two people. Even if people don't like you, they feel compelled, under these circumstances, to talk to you out of a sense of courtesy. I was worried about that girl, probably out for a walk, or sitting in her room reading some backpacker fiction or other. Maybe, though, she was like me and wanted to be left alone. After all, she was on her own also and perhaps preferred it that way. I was quite sure the hostel owner had already realised that I wasn't going to play cards with her in the living room, or take a guitar from my rucksack and sing some hippy songs into the fireplace.

Still, I felt almost paralyzed at the thought of bumping into either of them, and so stayed in my room for most of the evening. I knew I would have to leave at some point to eat. I was by now extremely hungry. I thought if I could hold out for a couple of hours longer, the Australian would be safely back in her room and I would have the kitchen to myself.

Eventually, at nine o'clock, I opened the door slowly and tiptoed down the hall, lit dimly by the light from the lobby. I realised that I had no idea where the kitchen was located. I stopped in my tracks to get my bearings and, at that precise moment, a door opened beside me, a rectangle of light spilling into the hallway. A young woman with blonde shoulder-length hair came out briskly. I stood perfectly still in the shadows, but as she pulled the door behind her she saw me.

'Jesus fucking Christ!' she exclaimed, her hand covering her mouth as she jumped back.

She stood there, catching her breath, then said: 'I'm sorry, mate. Didn't realise there was anyone else around the place.' She smiled, regaining her composure. 'Well, I'm Suzanna.'

'Hello,' I managed to mumble in response.

'Guess you're hungry too then.'

I stared at her for a moment, unsure what she meant. 'No. Not really. I was just...'

She looked down at my hands. In my panic I had forgotten I was holding a bag of pasta and a jar of pesto sauce.

'I guess we're having pasta then.'

'Ah, yes,' I managed, forcing a smile.

'Great. I'll show you to the kitchen then. Plain out of supplies. I'll cook though. You know, to make it up to you, mate.'

I stared at her in bafflement. She seemed to expect me to say something.

'Okay then, follow me,' she said. 'Suzanna,' she reiterated her name with the same broad smile on her face, I think in the hope that I would offer mine. I didn't. She turned and started to walk towards the foyer. I looked about in some last vain attempt to find a way out of the situation.

She turned around. 'Coming then?'

'Yes,' I said, uncertainly.

I followed her down the hallway, noticing only then how tall she was as she walked, all loose limbs and elbows, in front of me. On the other side of the foyer, the fluorescent lights flickered on to reveal a spacious kitchen separated from the lounge area by a counter. On one wall there was a large poster of a beach and, on another, a montage of postcards pinned to a notice board. A guitar leaned against the wall in the far corner by a beanbag, along with some bongos, a bodhrán and a tin whistle.

'You play?' she asked, gesturing towards them.

'No.'

'Pity. Neither do I.'

I was thankful for that, at least. Suzanna busied herself in the kitchen, opening cupboards and drawers. She seemed to know her way about the place – where the pots were, the salt, the herbs… I guessed she had been staying for a time.

Who knows how long. A week? A month? Wasn't the point of this sort of thing to keep moving – to keep running away from yourself for as long as possible?

'Okay then. Let's see what we've got here,' she said, more to herself than to me, as she lit the gas of the stove and began to fill a pot with water.

\*

Why Ireland?

Before my parents were divorced, we had been on holidays here. My mother didn't want to go, but my father insisted. I was young at the time. Seven or eight, I think. I couldn't confirm the year precisely because my mother refused to talk about it ever again. Anything that included my father was strictly out of bounds, and I finally relented and stopped asking her questions about Ireland. In fact, I stopped asking questions of any sort. Even I was a moody teenager once.

I don't remember the things one would expect a boy of that age to recall: the trip on the plane; the excitement of seeing another city apart from Bern. Like my mother (though I hate to admit it) I may also have chosen to forget most of that holiday. I think there were days when my parents hardly spoke to each other; and days when they only spoke in raised voices. I may be working backwards though (like a detective in a novel) from what was to come later, which I do remember, but deliberately avoid thinking about. Perhaps we were happy during those weeks, though I very much doubt it.

I do have one vivid recollection, though. There was a beach. I can hardly remember what it looked like or even where it was. I just remember that there was sand and the sea somewhere nearby crashing against the rocks. And that smell I had never experienced before: the sharp tang of seaweed and salt that caught you in the nose and lungs each time you took a breath.

In any case, what stays in my mind was not so much the beach as my father. I think of it now as a photograph in which there were only the two of us looking straight at the camera, smiling beside a sand castle. And, this being an imaginary photograph, it doesn't require that there be someone else behind the camera pressing the button. That person would have had to be, after all, my mother.

Soon after, when my father remarried, there were always other faces crowded into the picture and I seemed to get lost in the background somehow, my forehead glimpsed from behind the wall of smiling faces, or a shoulder intruding on an otherwise perfect family portrait.

But none of that had happened yet. My father and I were together, that was the important thing. I had never seen him so happy. We built – well, he built – a sandcastle with stones for windows and sticks for a drawbridge over the moat, which he padded with plastic so that the water wouldn't sink through the sand. He was an engineer, after all, so even our sandcastle had an attention to detail that surely other children would have envied if there had been any to see it. When he had finished, he used a piece of driftwood to write 'Castle Hermann' in big, Gothic letters on the sand in front of it.

And then the thing I will never forget. My father kneeled down beside me in the sand and asked in a low, mysterious voice, 'Where is an *inch* a *mile*, Hermann?'

I knew it was a riddle and all children love riddles. I thought about it hard, but I didn't understand it properly. What was an *inch* or a *mile* for that matter? This was typical of my father. He would often leave out crucial bits of information when giving you a problem to solve. A pattern

I noticed he increasingly resorted to after he left my mother.

I remembered another riddle that I had read in a book (or maybe heard in the playground) and gave the answer to that one because it seemed to make sense. 'Nowhere,' I said, a little unsurely.

He smiled.

'Good try but you're wrong!'

He looked out at the sea for a long moment, then turned to me and said, 'We are standing, right this very minute, Hermann, in the only place in whole wide world where an *inch* is a *mile*.'

He laughed and this time I laughed also.

'And that's where you'll find Castle Hermann if you ever need to see it again.'

Looking back on it now, I think that he was – how can I put it? – *lighter* than I'd ever seen him. Maybe he had already met Maria and knew this would be our last holiday together. That would explain why my parents fought so much during those weeks; why there was so much silence also. I am speculating of course. Parents never tell you the things that you need to know – never without trying to make themselves seem like the one who was betrayed or wronged. Who can say for sure what happened? I used to believe in certainties. When I discovered the truth – that all people, including my parents, were unpredictable and liable to lie to suit their purpose – I stopped believing in anything at all.

*

When I left Switzerland I was surprised how hard it was to find a place to live in Dublin. I spent a week in a cheap hotel before I found an apartment on the top storey of a Georgian house in a good part of town. It was small, but I liked the high ceilings with the cornices still intact, though they had been badly neglected. Two tall windows looked out onto the street, the top of a cherry blossom tree – just coming into flower – shifting uneasily in the breeze in the garden. The room was painted magnolia – a feature I had noticed in most flats I viewed – and had a cheap table and chair pushed against the wall by the window. The bedroom, to the back, was small, as was the bathroom.

At first I couldn't find the kitchen until, eventually, I realised it was the cupboard near the door. I opened it to find a small electric cooker and a tiny fridge. I rarely cooked and realised I would cook even less here.

Still, I liked my new habitat. It was more cramped than my apartment in Zurich, but its Spartan emptiness suited my new sense of things: simple, pared back, the bare walls empty of all associations. A good place for a new start, I thought. Yes, it would do.

I pulled the chair out and opened the window sash to allow some air into the room. The street seemed quiet. An occasional car passed, making its way towards the junction at the top of the road. A middle-aged woman in a blue overcoat walked a labrador, who pulled at the lead and stopped at every tree to relieve himself. I watched her as she made her slow progress up the road and finally out of view as she turned onto a side street pulling the dog behind her.

I stood up and began to unpack the two suitcases that rested on the wooden floor by the door.

I had no intention of working in those first weeks in Ireland. I had too much to think about. I could get a job later. In any case, I had plenty of money in the bank, though given how I had spent my entire adult life thinking about it, I found I rarely did so . I had to try to understand what had happened that day in the park. I simply couldn't go on unless I made sense of it. It would take as long as it would take. Three months, I imagined, should suffice. It was, after all, a big question: why on one day a cloud was just something floating above you, that you didn't notice and that didn't matter to you in the slightest; and on another it was... well, something else entirely. What, I couldn't say. That was the problem.

When I arrived in Ireland, my English was adequate. No, good is more accurate. In my teens I had read the novels of Sir Walter Scott, and I was a good student. I was particularly fond of *Ivanhoe* and perhaps this accounts for my somewhat formal style – though it is also true to say that my German was also very proper. Early in my adolescence I had realised that it was the best way to say very little, though I had also discovered it was a bad way to make friends – of either sex.

I spent the first three months in Dublin trying to knock the edges off my accent by listening to the radio. I tuned in to Pat Kenny each morning and would repeat phrases he said, trying each time to correct my inflection or mispronunciations. His voice was easy to understand, quite neutral in a way. I also found it comforting somehow to listen to people phone in and talk, though often I found it difficult to understand what they said, or follow discussions on local housing or political issues. (In those days I didn't realise that Fianna Fáil and Fine Gael were different parties.) Still, I liked to listen to these voices as they echoed through my empty room. Somehow they made me feel less alone.

Above all, in those first months, I hated the idea that people would think of me as a tourist. And perhaps, even more, I hated the idea that people would think of me as Swiss at all. When my English was fluent, I deliberately avoided thinking in German. I believed I could make the person I was disappear completely. I actually thought it would be that easy.

I had also discovered the answer to my father's riddle. On my second or third day I had bought a map of Dublin. (I never carried it with me, but would memorise the route to whatever place I wanted to visit. Only tourists, after all, carried maps.) 'Where is an *inch* a *mile*?' he had asked. The answer was simple: 'On a map.' That was the scale they used here. I had forgotten that the Irish still used a non-metric system. It was something I would have to get used to.

I was a little disappointed, though, that the answer had been so easy, and wondered why I hadn't thought of it before. I suppose I expected something more profound. Still, I had been only seven (or was it eight?) at the time and my father was just trying to entertain me. I would have liked to phone him with the answer, but he had died from cancer three years earlier.

*

Things started well in my new life. Most afternoons I would go to a nearby café – it was called *Au Lait* for some reason – and read. Or, I should say, study. I made notes, wrote on the margins (something I never did as a student) and started a filing system to order my thoughts. I wanted to go unnoticed but the café owner, Brian, a rotund man in early middle age, would often make idle conversation as he brought me my coffee, and I had told him my name. My birth name that is. There was no hiding the fact, in those early days, that I was not Irish. Apart from my landlord, he was the only person who knew it was Hermann. And there was no going back with him. In the end, I didn't mind so much that he knew. I liked him and he liked me enough to offer me free coffee from time to time, but I always declined his offer.

'Why won't you take it, Hermann?' he asked one afternoon. 'On the house. If you didn't spend so much money, sure we'd be on our backs.'

'Thank you. I appreciate the offer,' I replied, 'but I have the money.'

'Whatever you say, Hermann. If it makes ya more comfortable. I'll buy you a pint someday maybe?'

'Perhaps,' I said in a way that was intended to give him little hope of such an outcome.

He persisted nonetheless, tried many times to follow up on this, but I always had an excuse. I began to realise, as I elaborated on an imaginary circle of friends, that lying is harder than telling the truth. You have to be consistent and make notes about that also. It was all getting rather complicated.

It annoyed me greatly that I still often dreamt in German. I took some pleasure in the fact that, after only six months, people often mistook my accent as Irish, though I could never manage to drop my *th's* as people so often do here. It annoyed me also that my name had not been something more generic – say Peter, or Michael, or even Karl.

I had noticed an elderly man in the café who often sat by the window smoking cigarettes. He would sit there for hours and when I looked up from whatever book I was reading, he would just stare out at the people in the street. He never read the newspaper or anything of that kind. I wondered if he was lonely.

Eventually Brian introduced us. His name was Niall.

BoI Dep. A/c
40 - Day
2.25%
DIRT ( 27% )

BANK OF IRELAND : SAVINGS ACCOUNTS

Save to Borrow
DD 's

Easy Saver
3.25% <5k

Monthly
3.5 <5k

Pension : Pensions
Life Cover / Serious

PPS / Payslip.
Passport

*Signed:* _____

*Dated:* _____

'Ah, our friend who is so fond of words,' he said, as Brian left our coffees on the table. 'What are you reading today?'

'Hegel,' I said.

'Um,' he said studying the cover of the book. 'Good?'

'In places. He makes some interesting arguments.'

'Yes. Well... Your name. I was wondering?'

'My mother was Swiss. Dead now,' I said, without a thought, though only one of these statements was true.

'Oh, I'm sorry to hear that. You grew up here then?'

'Yes,' I replied, happy that I had passed some kind of test I had set myself.

We sat for some time in silence, Niall watching the street as usual. Outside a young Asian woman stopped and adjusted her hair in the reflection of the glass, then walked on. I had noticed her before. She worked in the second-hand bookshop down by the canal that I occasionally visited, and sometimes came to the coffee shop after work.

Niall turned to me and asked in his quiet, lilting voice, 'Are you a teacher, then?'

'No.' I thought for a moment. 'I'm writing a book.'

'Makes sense. I wish you luck with it.'

I was surprised at how easy it was to sustain the illusion. He didn't ask me any further questions; no attempt to elicit personal information, or discover what this fictitious book was supposed to be about. He stood up and put on his tweed jacket.

'Well, Hermann, it was nice meeting you.'

He shook my hand firmly.

'Good luck with your book. I'm sure you will have an interesting story to tell.'

I wanted to correct him. I certainly had no intention of writing a story, but he was making his way towards the door already. What, after all, would such a book be about, if I should ever write one?

I didn't see Niall in the café again, and some months later Brian told me that he had died from cancer.

'I'm sorry to hear that,' I said. I felt genuine sadness, which surprised me given that I hardly knew him. 'He seemed like an interesting man.'

'Yes, he was. A very good man. Gentleman. You know, he was a professor of theology at Trinity College. Before he became too ill to teach, that is.'

'Really. He never mentioned.'

'Not his style, Hermann. Bit like you in that regard.'

As I walked the streets that night in the cold and the rain, I couldn't help but wonder why Niall never read any books in all those hours sitting by the window. Had he read them all already? The ones that mattered. He didn't appear to have known Hegel, which was a surprising omission. I regretted not asking him for some recommendations. He might have saved me a lot of time in the area of theological debate. (I had recently wasted much time on this topic.) I had been in Ireland for nearly a year. I felt no closer to the solution of my problem, and I found that I had again developed that tiredness in my eyes, which I had first noticed that day before the meeting with François and Silka.

I hadn't been sleeping lately.

*

Some weeks later, I found myself walking along the canal bank trying to build up the courage to go to the second-hand bookshop. I stopped at the door, then pushed it open, a bell ringing as I went through. I glanced towards the counter to where the young Asian woman sat. She looked up from her book and smiled, then looked down again.

I browsed the 'Irish Interest' section and pretended to read the jacket notes. A man in his early forties with long greying hair and a beard placed an armful of paperbacks on the counter.

'Hi! How are you today?' she asked, again with that fleeting smile.

'Ah, not bad, Tien. And yourself?'

'I am very well, thank you.'

'Busy?'

'Yes. Not now, but earlier yes.'

'Good, good. And how are the studies?' he asked, gesturing towards the book she was reading.

'Oh, very good. I start my exams soon. Have to study harder.' She laughed shyly, then picked up the first paperback and tapped in the price on the cash register. 'Colin Dexter again. You enjoy this Colin Dexter!'

'Like a good thriller, you know. Keep the pages turning and all that!'

He handed her a note and she smiled again as she gave him his change.

'Well, I'll see you again, Tien. When I've got through this lot.'

'When all the pages have been turned, yes?' she said, laughing nervously at her own joke. The man laughed out loud.

'Exactly! When all the pages are turned,' he said. 'Well, see you again.'

As he opened the door and disappeared into the street, I glanced down the aisle. The shop was empty apart from the Asian woman – well, Tien, as I now knew her name to be. I picked up the first book on the top of the pile and approached the counter.

'Hi!' Tien said.

'Hello,' I replied. I wanted to say something more but couldn't, and just watched as she checked the price on the inside cover and tapped it into the register.

'Seven euros fifty cent please,' she said.

I rummaged in my pocket trying to find the exact change. Finally, I placed it on the counter. She handed me the book in a bag and smiled.

'Thank you.'

I stood there for a moment. Her smile faded as she looked down towards her textbook. Though it was upside down from my perspective I instantly recognized the cascading lines of calculus. She was studying macro-economic modelling.

She glanced up from her book and finally I spoke: 'I was wondering, if… well, if perhaps you would like to go for a coffee sometime? I see you in *Au Lait* sometimes. Maybe we could go there?'

Her brow furrowed. 'I'm sorry, I don't understand – '

'It's just I thought you might remember me. I come in here sometimes… '

'I don't remember. I'm sorry,' she said quietly, her face flushing.

I felt like an actor on stage who had forgotten his lines, his heart pounding as the audience stared at him in silence.

'I have boyfriend already,' she continued. 'I'm sorry.'

The bell of the door rang as a woman and a young child came in.

'No, I'm sorry,' I blurted, then stumbled away from the counter. The bell rang again as I came out onto the street, dazed. As I walked by the window, I glanced in and saw the woman talking to Tien. Tien smiled, said something then walked towards a bookcase. I watched her for a moment as she took a book from the shelf. She glanced towards the window and I turned away, walking briskly out of her view and up the street towards the café. I needed a strong coffee after failing my audition so miserably.

*

Books. So many books. I had started with the philosophers. Kant. Spinoza. Nietzsche. But there was something missing. The clouds I had seen that day in the park were not there. I read books on science. Books on sociology. On psychology. On anthropology; on mythology, biology, physics... But it all seemed so incomplete and contradictory. Had I the ear or eye for such things, I might have found what I was searching for in great art or poetry. But I was a logical man even when I knew I was applying logic to things that were – it was becoming increasingly apparent – far from reasonable.

One day as I sat in the café staring into my half-empty cup of coffee, I had a strange thought. Perhaps *I* was the thing that was missing; that the only moment I ever truly existed was that moment under the clouds on a cold day in April.

I had begun to think increasingly of those moments in the park as a curse. I was like the man I had read about in a newspaper article who had received the most moving and passionate love letter in the post, but found that there was no name or return address on either the letter or envelope. He had spent his life trying to find this woman and never succeeded in his quest. Those clouds were like that for me: if that day had never happened, I would be content, in a fashion, and still working for a bank in Zurich. I would have been promoted several times by now and would probably be François's senior and would make him refer to Frau Libnovsky as Silka. But there was no going back to that world and I had no world to go forward into. I was beginning to feel lost. I was drowning again. Yes, I was beginning to drown.

\*

The empty plates lay before us on the table. We hardly spoke throughout the meal. It was adequate I suppose, but I couldn't understand why she had added tomato purée to a perfectly good pesto sauce. There wouldn't be another meal but, if there had been, I would have insisted on doing the cooking, though, in truth, I hadn't cooked in a very long time.

'You're a man of few words,' Suzanna said at last.

I was snapped from my thoughts again.

'Yes,' I replied.

There was another awkward pause. I felt guilty and self-conscious about my manners. Or lack of them.

'I'm sorry. I know people sometimes find it uncomfortable,' I said.

'No. That's not what I meant. I like it. I'm a man of too many words as you've probably noticed.'

That smile again, as though I were supposed to react in some way.

'It was a joke…' she said, trailing off.

I hate it when I miss jokes. People think you are stupid instead of abstracted. She persisted, self-conscious now herself (an effect I also noticed I had on people): '*Man of few words* … I just meant…'

'Yes I understand. I don't say much.'

'No. Not that. That doesn't bother me – that's all I was trying to say. Maybe if you gave me some of your silences,

36

and I gave you some of my words, we'd both be happier with ourselves.'

'I'm afraid you may have misunderstood. I hadn't meant to give you the impression – '

'Shit, I'm sorry. I didn't mean to suggest anything,' she said, beginning to regret, I suspected, having cornered me for dinner in the first place.

'Well, yes,' I said.

Another pause, longer than all those that preceded it.

'Christ, you are hard work, mate. Anyone ever told you that?'

'Not so bluntly.' I pushed my chair back and stood up. 'Maybe I should leave.'

'No don't,' she said, with a hint of remorse. 'I wasn't saying that. I mean, I like a challenge.'

'I won't tell you anything,' I said, softening a little. I picked up the plates and cutlery and brought them to the sink.

'Is *that* a challenge?'

'No,' I said, rinsing the sauce from the ceramic.

She stood beside me. 'Okay then. Where do you live?'

I didn't want to say anything but knew she wouldn't get far.

'Dublin,' I said.

'Good start. You see, not that hard. Okay. What do you work at?'

That caught me out a little. I needed a cover story. I fumbled for a knife in the sink.

'Eh, well, I'm writing a book.'

She took a dishcloth from the counter and began drying the plates. 'Great. Feel free to, you know, elaborate.'

'I never talk about what I'm working on. As a rule.'

'Okay. But from this I can deduce that you have written other books. What are *they* about?'

'What?' I said, slightly panicked. People never persist beyond a certain point. At least, not with me.

'This isn't your first book?'

'Yes. Yes it is.'

'You said – '

'I said I never talk about what I'm working on.'

'Exactly. The word "never" implies a pattern. A habit. Previous books.'

'I don't think so.' Damn it, she was right.

'Well, you are something of a mystery man.'

'Quite the opposite,' I replied, and meant it.

'I'm not going to ask you your name by the way, mate. That seems to be a state secret. In its absence I'm just going to call you, well, let's see.' She pretended to think for a moment. 'Mate! For the rest of the weekend. I'm going to do this till I break you down… mate.'

I decided to ignore her new and annoying approach. I suspected that even if she knew my name she would refer to me as mate anyway.

She filled the kettle. 'Tea then, mate?'

'No. I never have caffeine after six. It stays in your system for twelve hours. Did you know that?'

'No. Fascinating. I'll bear that in mind.' She lit the gas and sat down.

A change of tactic was required. I realised, from situations like this in the past, that the best form of defence is attack. Oldest trick in the book, in fact. Usually I had used this only in desperate predicaments as a diversionary stratagem. This time I found, despite myself, that I was beginning to be vaguely curious about my enemy.

'So, what do *you* do?' I asked.

'Well, mate, I'm an Australian backpacker.'

'No, I meant…'

'I know what you meant. As I was saying …'

'Okay. I get it.' I tried again. 'So where have you been to on your travels so far?'

'Never talk about it. Some people like to tell long, interesting stories about the fascinating and strange people they meet in other hostels in far-flung, exotic countries. But, you know, I *never* do that. Wrecks the mystique, I think, that the backpacker aspires to. As a *rule.*'

'Ha!' I exclaimed triumphantly. 'You used the word "never" so you have given some information away. By your own logic, it means you have backpacked before.'

'I've never backpacked before,' she said flatly, 'mate.'

The kettle reached the boil in the background, a slight hiss rising to a pitched note. I could see she was enjoying herself. I was beginning to like this game too. No disclosure; no personal revelations; no *I'll tell you my life story if you tell me yours.* Why can't every conversation be like this, I wondered.

'Well,' I said. 'I suppose the one comfort I can draw from your approach to – what was it you said, "preserving your mystique"? – is that you will never tell anyone else in some other hostel in some far flung corner of the world, about me.'

'Definitely not. Lips are sealed. Your secret's safe with me, mate.'

Suzanna got up from her chair and lifted the kettle from the cooker. 'Cup of hot water, then?'

'Is there chamomile, by any chance?'

'Huh, another clue. I'm beginning to build a picture,' she said.

'What?'

'I'm guessing insomniac. Am I right?'

'Absolutely not,' I replied with the speed of a pathological liar, a trait I suspected she had already noticed. 'Must go to bed. It's getting late.'

'It's 11 o'clock!'

'Nevertheless.' I stood up. 'Well, thank you for dinner.'

'You're welcome. My pleasure. Must do it again sometime,' she replied, flatly.

I walked past her towards the door to the foyer.

'I'm guessing you're not even Irish, mate?'

'What?' I said, alarmed.

She craned her head around: 'I'm guessing you're at least half English.'

'Right. Well, good night then,' I said, disguising my relief.

'Good night then,' she said turning her back to me again, 'Edward.'

\*

Brian finally cornered me for a drink. I had met him in the street by accident. Ireland was to play Switzerland in an important football match. I didn't like football much, but I had intended to go to a pub and pretend to be a Michael or a Peter and hide in the crowd and maybe have a pint of Guinness. (I had never acquired the taste for it, but sometimes I just liked the look of it on the table in front of me.)

'Going to watch the match?' he asked.

'Yes.' It had just come out before I could think of anything to say.

'Good. Let's watch it together. I can buy you that drink. Slattery's have a grand screen. Big one.'

'I was supposed to meet friends.'

'Too late. You'll miss the kick-off. I won't take no for an answer. You have, after all, been my pension plan, Hermann. It's the least I could do.'

'Well…' I doddered, unable to think of an excuse quickly enough. That was another thing about lying: you had to appear to be absolutely certain. This often meant saying the first thing that came into your head. With strangers it was easy. With Brian I had to cross-reference my previous lies and that took time. I had delayed too long.

'Settled then. You can phone your friends from the pub,' he said.

I don't know if it was a good match really, but that didn't matter to me. The match mattered for other reasons that were bigger than football. Neither team had scored. In the closing minutes, an Irish player had fouled a Swiss player near the box. The whole pub moaned. The Swiss player (was it Cellestini?) placed the ball on the ground, then walked away from it slowly as the referee pushed the Irish players back several metres. The pub was completely silent. Cellestini stood for a long time. Everything was still. He ran casually towards the ball, then struck it hard. It seemed to hang in the air for a long time, as though the whole thing was a replay in slow motion. Everyone in the crowded bar held their breath. The ball then suddenly sped up before dipping at the last moment and crashing into the top corner of the net. There was a different kind of silence in the pub, then. I heard someone groan from another table and explode, 'For fuck's sake! Bleedin' arseholes! Where was the wall? Jesus Christ!'

I didn't make a sound.

Afterwards, Brian shook my hand and said, 'Well done, Hermann. Ye deserved it on the day. No complaints. Fair result.'

I was stunned. 'What do you mean?' I asked. 'We lost.'

He looked back at me with a baffled expression on his face, then said, somewhat unconvincingly, 'Fair play to ya, son.' I hadn't understood what he meant.

Then, as I put my coat on: 'You look a little pale, Hermann. Have ya been eatin' right?'

'Yes. Certainly,' I retorted, though in truth, I couldn't remember when I had last eaten a proper meal.

I didn't go back to the café again, or see Brian (which was difficult given how close I lived to the place). Well, only once, and that was nearly a year later.

*

One day in December, or was it January? I can't properly remember. So many things have become blurred. Well, let me say then: one day in winter, I lay on a table in a dimly lit room. Candles burned around me and the air was thick with incense. A woman stood above me mumbling a strange chant as she placed coloured stones along the length of my chest. As each one touched my skin, the cold, hard surface made me suddenly twitch. I saw her hand reach for a large pink crystal on a tray beside her. She lowered it slowly onto my forehead. She said it would make my thoughts calm, that I would understand everything in time. Then she left the room.

I lay on the table, the heavy crystal above my eyes pressing down on my thoughts, the incense catching in my nose, making me feel that I couldn't breathe. The flickering of the candles brought only fear as my heart raced and the stones on my chest rose and fell to its panicked rhythm, then tumbled to the floor.

When she returned I was sitting on the edge of the table, shaking. She said again that, in time, I would understand, but I knew I wouldn't. Not here. Not in this room. There was something missing. I put on my shirt and paid her, then left without saying a word.

And the more I tried to find that missing piece of the puzzle, the further I seemed to move away from the thing I wanted most: to be in that park again and to look up and have my heart blown open – to have again that same feeling, that weightlessness and comfort of the moment of beauty just before the moment of fear that followed and from which, it seemed, I couldn't escape.

In the weeks following my visit to the woman who placed stones along the length of my body, I tried many other things (each more desperate in turn) and which I will not catalogue for fear of embarrassment. My confusion seemed to grow a little more each day. I had that vague sensation of falling that people often experience as they are about to sleep. It just didn't stop and I was afraid that the fear itself would never stop. The feeling grew a little stronger every day, until it felt like I was plummeting from a great height with nothing to stop me falling further, even the hard sudden impact of water or concrete, which might have seemed like a relief under the circumstances.

*

One morning I awoke to the sound of shouting. I climbed out of bed and edged towards the door and pressed my ear against the cold surface. I could hear my mother screaming, over and over, 'How long has this being going on? How long? Tell me, how long?'

When I went outside, I saw a large suitcase lying on the polished wood of the landing. My father came from the bedroom with another. When he saw me he stopped and stared, an anguished look in his eyes. He was about to speak when my mother came from the room and threw a blue shirt at him.

'You can take that as well. I don't want any of your belongings in my home.'

It was then she saw me.

'If I have my way, you'll never see the boy again, you hear me?'

I began to cry. My mother rushed forward and took my hand. My father said nothing, just looked towards the shirt on the floor and slowly picked it up. After a moment, he took the suitcases in his hands and walked slowly down the staircase, turning at the bottom to glance up at me.

Later, my mother gathered all his remaining possessions in the garden and burnt them. As the smoke plumed above the flames, I noticed a photograph of my parents on the ground. I picked it up, the heat from the fire reddening my face. They were standing in front of a church on a piazza somewhere in Italy, the sun shining down on them like a benediction. My mother's right hand was raised to shield the light from her eyes, and with the other she held my father's hand tightly. They looked so young and happy standing there, as though the future could bring only happiness to their lives.

My mother pulled the picture from my hand roughly and threw it into the flames. The image seemed to float momentarily before the photograph curled at the edges and ignited with a blue-green flame, then vanished forever.

'You're my little man now,' she said. 'You must promise me you'll never leave me like your father. Promise me, Hermann. And I will love you. Promise me and I will love you.'

I promised, but from the moment she asked for my love, I was unable to give it. It was conditional on me hating my father, and I could never hate him, though I knew what he did was wrong. I tried to be a good son, but it was never

44

good enough. In some way, she would always end up comparing me to him. As time went on I grew to like the comparison.

In truth, I wasn't like my father. His silences gave him an allure I never possessed. My silences were that of the dumbfounded. I had just grown numb after he left. It was easier that way: to say nothing in that joyless house, where words had become a form of allegiance, or betrayal.

*

After my meal with Suzanna, I returned to my room. I packed my bag, then sat on the edge of the bed. Despite my long walk that morning with a heavy rucksack, I felt no fatigue. Or maybe it is more correct to say that I was so tired I was beyond sleep, as had so often been the case. I had some Chinese herbal remedy with me that I had bought in a health food store before I left.

I took the small, green bottle from my travel bag and read the instructions. Forty drops in a glass of water. I looked at the bedside table. The ceramic jug was empty. I would have to go to the kitchen again.

I waited, then opened the door quietly. I thought Suzanna would have gone to bed, but I heard her voice echoing from the lobby. I listened carefully. At first I thought she was talking to herself, but then realised she was on the phone. I decided to fill the jug in the bathroom instead and walked slowly down the corridor trying to make as little noise as possible.

I stopped at the door of the bathroom and could hear Suzanna talking, though she was hidden from my view.

She laughed out loud, then said, 'I miss you too, Dad.'

There was no sadness, though, in the way she said it. It was casual and warm.

'Yeah, Dad, I know. I love you too. I'll talk to you when I get back to Dublin.'

Another pause, then, 'Hi Mom! Yeah, I'm great. I'm at the Dingle Peninsula…. Oh, yeah. It's so beautiful here, Mom. You really have to see it sometime. The sea is amazing. So different than back home.'

She was silent for a moment, then, 'Yeah, I'm going to stay here for a few more days… Well, it's a bit cold but I didn't come here for the weather.'

She laughed again, and listened. 'Well, I start in two weeks… I'm *so* excited, Mom. I met my supervisor before I came down here and he seemed like a really top bloke… Said that the marine habitats here are very different, but that I wouldn't have a problem catching up…'

I pushed the door to the bathroom and walked inside, Suzanna's words becoming a jumbled echo against the tiles as the door closed with a thud behind me. I didn't want her to think I had been listening in. I turned on the tap and filled the jug noisily, then placed it on the edge of the hand basin. I put the plug in and filled the basin with the hot water tap, then washed my face and hands.

I opened the door and walked out into the hall. I glanced towards the lobby and saw Suzanna standing there, lost in her thoughts. I wondered if she had been crying, as she stared at the floor. I turned and walked towards my room.

'Goodnight, mate,' she said after me, though this time quietly.

I stopped and turned. I looked at her for a moment, standing there alone, her blonde hair falling across her face.

'Goodnight,' I replied and smiled, then walked down the darkened corridor towards my room.

\*

I had been walking the streets. I would get up and sit by the window for hours looking out onto the cherry blossom swaying just below me in the garden, watching the people pass by the railing going somewhere or returning home. Sometimes I just listened to the rain as it tapped against the glass, the world outside blurry and distorted as the raindrops streaked down the windowpane. When I could bear no more of the tedium, I would force myself to dress and leave the flat and walk. Just walk. I thought if maybe I could go far enough, for long enough, I might tire myself and sleep.

The things I had found fresh and different when I first arrived now had the same jaded, hollow feeling I had experienced that day in Zurich: the flea market on George's Street; Stephen's Green with its with people in suits eating lunch, so like that park I had crossed two years before. Even the Georgian grandeur of Trinity College seemed like a faded imitation of some grander institution in England. The red brick of the houses on Merion Square, smut-grimed and depressing to me now.

The qualities I once enjoyed in the people began to grate also – the way they carelessly threw a cigarette butt onto the pavement, or crossed a street against the traffic lights. All that banter and easy charm felt like a casual disregard. It was my old self surfacing in me. I knew that. But I could only see fault in all the places and people I thought would mark a new beginning; that I wanted so dearly to become part of, that I had sacrificed my own accent for.

But I didn't fit in. Not here, not anywhere. I just kept walking the city streets waiting for a jolt, a moment of inclusion, of being there in the street and feeling like I belonged in this place. On the Ha'Penny Bridge, I watched the faces passing, jostling in a swarm as they finished work and made their way towards buses that would undoubtedly be late. I looked at them – men and women of all ages, the teenagers with their baggy jeans and piercings – and I felt nothing. They were just a catalogue of expressions as they passed, the snatches of their conversations a babble to my ears.

I wanted to float above it all and look down and see some pattern: to see some purpose in the heave of people; in the line of buses idling on the Quays; in the rows of cars stuck in traffic. But a great weight was pressing down on me, fixing me to this spot as the faces continued by me on their restless errands.

I returned to my flat as the day grew dark. I was exhausted and was certain I would sleep. As I opened the door I stopped in my tracks, shocked. It was the closest moment I had to that day in Zurich – except in reverse. I felt fear, though not because of beauty, but because I saw the chaos I had become. The walls were cluttered with notes, pictures and diagrams, with schematics that I no longer understood. There were bags of papers, clippings, leads, false trails.... There were books piled in every corner of the room. Dirty plates, cups, and dishes were strewn about the floor. There was the sharp, sweet smell of milk that has gone off.

The room had the appearance of a home that had been ransacked by thieves who had tossed everything about in their attempt to find the secret place where the money was hidden. And the more desperate they became, the more difficult their task to find anything in the disarray they were causing. If I had not been so shocked, I might have sensed the metaphor: that a good thief would move one thing at a time, always replacing it to its original location, not so that his theft would go undetected, but that his search would be calm and systematic. Perhaps though, that is how all robberies begin and my flat was how all robberies look when they're finished.

*

The room in the hostel had grown cold as I sat looking out the window. Outside, by the gravel path, the yellow heads of the daffodils quivered on their stems. The crepuscular light of early morning seemed to be trapped in their fragile petals, and illuminated them as though from within. The oak trees near the gate stood like charcoal sketches against the pale sky beyond them.

I put on my trousers and shirt, and a heavy woollen jumper. I packed my rucksack with things I didn't need. Books mainly, though I hardly read . I put on my coat and opened the door slowly, trying not to make a sound.

I tiptoed down the corridor as I had done the night before. This time I stopped at Suzanna's door deliberately. I stood there listening. She was probably still asleep. I wondered what she might be dreaming of. I was curious about other people's dreams since I appeared to no longer have any of my own.

As I opened the front door of the hostel, I heard footsteps behind me. I turned. The owner walked into the lobby in a bathrobe, drying her hair with a towel. She looked up and saw me.

'Guten morgen,' she said, brightly.

'Guten morgen,' I replied by instinct, in a perfect German accent. I opened the door, wanting to flee.

'Peter. I had not understood zat you vere German. But Kostik. Yes. Zis is a German name.'

'I'm not German,' I said bluntly, then walked out the door and down the gravel pathway.

'You vill be having breakfist?' she called after me.

'No,' I shouted back, without turning, and just kept walking towards the gate past all those daffodils quivering against the green of the lawn.

\*

I received a letter in the post. The only mail I got was from the bank. I would open these statements, put them down somewhere, and usually even forget to read them. This one caught my attention, though. It was the first time in my life that I had received a financial document with red ink on it. I was in debt.

I found myself again at the door of the *Au Lait* after nearly a year of avoiding it. I hovered there on the street, wondering if I should go in. Just as I decided that it was a bad idea, Brian's face – slightly redder than I had remembered – appeared.

'Ah, Hermann!' he said with real warmth. 'Come in, come in.'

I hesitated, then said quietly, 'Thank you, Brian.'

I sat at the window table and after a couple of minutes he brought a coffee to me.

'On the house. I insist.'

'Thank you,' I said.

'Good! Good,' he replied, clearly surprised. He smiled, then returned to the counter where a young man stood waiting to pay.

I sat there for some time sipping on the coffee. I had to make it last. My thoughts were racing. I was trying to build myself up for something that I had never done before, never imagined I would have to do. Finally, I went to the counter.

'Well, Hermann, it's great to see you back. You were away?' Brian asked, as he took a tray of cups from the washer, the steam rising towards his face.

'Yes, I was away.' It was true in a sense.

'How's the health?' he asked, as direct as ever.

'Not great really.'

'Well, if you ever need anything…'

'I do… need something.' The words caught in my throat, but I had said them at last.

'Oh. Go on,' he said.

'It's embarrassing really. I don't know how to ask – '

'How much?' he said, without fuss, as he dried his hands.

'It's just that I need a holiday, I think. A couple of days away somewhere.'

'Will five hundred cover you?'

'Yes. That would be very kind. More than enough really.'

'Where are you going? I mean, if it's to go home ye'll need more than that, surely.'

'No. Just somewhere in Ireland. Away from the city.'

'Kerry's the place. Beautiful down there. You'll love it.'

'Yes, I've heard…'

'Dingle Peninsula,' he continued. 'Most beautiful place in the whole country.' He disappeared into the storeroom. When he got back a few minutes later, he discretely handed me an envelope.

'Consider it a gift.'

'No. I must pay you back,' I insisted.

'Well. If you must. Whenever you have it. No rush. Business has been good lately.'

When I returned to the flat, I felt quite low. Having to ask for money like that was very difficult for me. No.

Unthinkable even. I went to sit down in the armchair but had to move papers and a bowl of half-eaten porridge to do so.

You might say my in-tray was full to overflowing. It was piled so high that I could not diminish it in ten lifetimes. (I had begun to think in terms of money again since I saw that red ink, and much of it was in German.) I had spent two years in that room on a quiet Dublin street. I was now thirty-three years old. Order had given way not to greater order but to an unstoppable entropy.

I could not even sit down to have a cup of tea to calm my shock without moving one pile of confusion onto another. Confusion piled upon confusion. I wondered if confusion could be added or subtracted, could balance itself out or just simply accrue like a bad debt. Hyper-inflationary self-delusion. The books were no longer balanced. François, if he could only see me now, might have a faint smile forming on his lips. *You are wrong* it would suggest, but he wouldn't say it. He would just look at me calmly, as I had done all those years before, and wait for me to come to the meeting before exposing my folly. But I would not come to his meeting or any other.

We were both wrong in our different ways. Was mine a more noble failure? People would have you believe so. The heroic quest. Unfulfilled, yes, but at least one tried. I found that I had come to disagree, had come to hate that nylon shoelace. 'Beauty,' I read somewhere, 'is the language of hope.' I had discovered it could also be the language of destruction. That was perhaps the one original thought I had had in my whole life. Beauty – if you are not ready for it – can drive you crazy, like that man who received the love letter, dying alone and bitter in a flat much like this, wondering in the end if he had written it himself and missed the purpose of the gesture.

As I stood on the beach, staring out at the sea, I thought of these things. All the clues I had missed along the way. All the chances I had squandered, each false move I had made. I had solved my father's riddle at last, but this didn't bring any consolation. The beach was called Inch Strand. I had read about it in a brochure I picked up in the hostel. I read and reread it, during the sleepless night, trying to find the significance. But it didn't matter . It was just a stupid story my father had told to amuse a child. A child who would be left behind, after all.

And then, like that footballer on the television, I just started walking, casually at first and then in a light run. The water sloshed about my feet, Inch Strand stretching for a mile behind me like a thin, ironic smile. In front of me was the Atlantic Ocean. There was land, of course, across a great distance. But such distances exist only on maps. I stood on the end of the world and I think I had intended to walk off its edge. What is the sea, if not a form of confusion so vast that it is perhaps beyond confusion?

So maybe I had intended to walk into it and disappear forever. But I hadn't expected the cold, the shock, as my calf muscles started to spasm and lock, the iron clad grip of my jeans fastening about my legs. I couldn't move. For some reason, I remembered that Ireland was surrounded by the Gulf Stream, which accounted largely for its moderate climate. But this didn't matter. It seemed even the sea didn't want me – would give me no passage. I looked out across the grey, swelling, endless muscle of it. I cried out. Words. I don't know what words. I screamed and heard myself shouting into the emptiness: 'Father, why didn't you take me with you?'

At that moment I heard a voice, as though it were a distant answer. I assumed it was in my head. It wouldn't have been the first time that I had heard things that weren't there. But there it was again.

'Mate!' A hand pulled me around. Suzanna stood there, the water nearly up to her chin.

She looked at me and said: 'Are you okay?'

I couldn't reply. I must have looked terrible, from the expression on her face.

She led me back to the beach, both us of shivering. I thought I might start crying, but I didn't. I wasn't sure I knew how to . It was as if my body had forgotten. We stood for a long time on the sand, shivering uncontrollably.

'Well, you're a... silly... bugger,' she said at last. 'Thought you were... trying to... kill yourself.'

Before I could answer, she laughed. A nervous laugh, I suppose. Laughed so hard that she bent over double. I couldn't muster a response, but I think I may have smiled faintly or possibly even properly.

'So, I'm Suzanna,' she said, as if we had never met. 'Who the hell... are you... mate?'

I stared straight at her and said, 'My name is... Hermann.'

'Hermann. Good name... Shouldn't be ashamed of it... Thought you'd never tell me. Thought we were going to have to play that... stupid game for the whole weekend.'

She looked at me for a moment – again that look – as though she expected me to say something.

'Well, Hermann, don't know about you but... I'm a bit fuckin'... chillers. Fancy a coffee?'

This time I laughed. Laughed as if I'd never heard such a ridiculous thing in my whole life as the word 'chillers'.

'Yes,' I managed, between what I can only describe as guffaws (a word I've never had a use for before and wondered why it existed). 'A coffee... would be nice.'

'Good. I think under the circumstances... this one's on you, mate.'

'Yes. I suppose it is.'

We walked up the strand in silence towards the coffee shop in the distance. There was no sunlight in the clouds. The sky was a blanket of nondescript grey, the sea a restless presence to our right. It was there. Just there. It was neither beautiful nor ugly. I felt something else entirely. I search now in two languages as I write, and find in the end the word that comes closest is *zärtlichkeit*. You could translate it as intimacy. Or maybe tenderness.

Or whatever word would describe this woman, Suzanna, who would wade into an ocean to touch a man on the shoulder to see if he was alright. A man whose name she didn't even know. I hadn't expected that. I thought I had disappeared so completely that I had become invisible to the world. That that was perhaps what I had wanted all along.

I was wrong.

# Our Friends Electric

# Just Can't Get Enough (3:43)

The only woman I ever loved stepped onto a plane four days before Christmas to leave this city forever. I wasn't there. Another bloke waved goodbye to her. I know his name. I'm not going to tell you it. Let's just call him Cecil for the time being. Suits him from what I've heard. Anyway, not sure I care about either of them , to tell you the truth.

Okay, so where did it start? Dame Street. June 25$^{th}$ 2009. 11.53 in the PM. Third date with Lisa. We were getting on really well. We'd met in a café two weeks earlier. We hadn't kissed yet. This was part of what I reckon made me attractive to her. I had behaved like a gentleman, which is apparently unusual these days, or so she kept telling me. Truth was, I was scared shitless of her. She was very attractive: tall; high cheekbones; long raven hair; all that other stuff. I'd lost my confidence with women some time ago. For most people *some time ago* might mean three to four weeks (from what Lisa was telling me), but in my case you can convert those weeks into years.

I also happened to like her a lot, which made me even more scared. She was just so damn intelligent. And funny. And the other stuff I just mentioned. I let her do most of the talking, which I think also helped my case. She liked music as well. I didn't know most of the stuff she listened to but that didn't matter. She *liked* music, that was the point. I mean *really* liked music. She even played in some band that I hadn't heard of, but I suspected that they must be pretty good from what she was saying. Anyway, we had a common passion. Or so I thought at the time.

We were sitting at the window table in Café Mocha, overlooking the street below and all the people hanging around the Hairy Lemon, joking and laughing in groups, leaning against walls, or sitting on the pavement with their pints. I looked at Lisa as she stirred the sugar into her decaf skinny latte.

'Do'ya have a keyboard player?' I asked, hoping she would say no because I had just bought a Yamaha PSR-S550 and was learning to play it (and had spent six months of hell working in a video shop to pay for the bloody thing).

She looked up from her cup and said thoughtfully, 'No. We prefer acoustic instruments. Purer sound?'

I was a bit taken aback by that. All sound was pure, in my opinion, particularly *non*-acoustic sound.

'The Yamaha PSR-S550 can sound like anything you want it to sound like,' I said encouragingly, 'even an orchestra if that's the kind of sound you're interested in bringing into the, yunno, mix or whatever.'

'Not the same,' she replied bluntly, and I could see she had maybe a strongish opinion on the subject.

I was always surprised when people considered electric guitars an 'acoustic' instrument, let alone electric basses. I let it go though because, as I said, I liked her and she seemed to like me back, so why break the circle of mutual interest and respect at this point, or any other for that matter.

'Sure. Whatever you're inta. You've gotta be comfortable with your sound. With your general, yunno, sonic texture.' I thought she'd dig that bit. 'That's the most important thing.'

'That's just… That's just such a nice thing to say. You're such a sweetheart. Most people don't realise just how important it is,' she said with what I'm pretty sure was an air of admiration.

'As I say, whatever you're inta. I'd love to hear your band sometime. Sound like you know what you're after. That's important too,' I added, following on from the success of my last comment.

'Yes. Very.'

She looked down at her latte again, then looked up at me across the red tabletop and smiled. It was weird the way she could do that. Smile and not blink. Yunno, the way people do it for photographs. I felt kinda intimidated in a way and grinned back for a moment, then looked down into my coffee, trying to think of something else to say.

Later we stood on Dame Street, after our third, hard session of cappuccino drinking. She leaned close to me and said: 'Had a really good time with you tonight. You're just so different from most of the guys I meet. I mean you're sensitive. Shit, I know that sounds like bollix but you are.'

Then she kissed me. I didn't really kiss back at first, because I was a bit scared at the pace of development in our relationship, but I threw caution to the wind and got into it. God it felt good though. I was quite overwhelmed by the whole thing really. I knew it was 11.53 because I still had my eyes open and I could see the clock outside the Stag's Head and all the people standing there with their pints looking at us. I closed my eyes at the exact moment she stopped, then rested her head on my shoulder.

I was a bit surprised by the silence and, I guess, I suddenly felt a little nervous. And when I feel nervous I tend to - one: talk; and two: fall back on other people's inspiration.

*'When I'm with you baby*
*I go out of my head*
*And I just can't get enough*
*And I just can't get enough*
*All the things you do to me*
*And everything you said*
*I just can't get enough*
*I just can't get enough...'*

Lisa looked up at me like she was about to speak, but I wanted to get the much better second verse in first...

*'We walk together*
*We're walking down the street*
*And I just can't get enough*
*And I just can't get enough*
*Every time I think of you*
*I know we have to meet*
*And I just can't seem to get enough of... you.'*

Lisa looked up into my face with those sparkling, corn-flower-blue eyes. 'That is *so* beautiful. Who wrote that?'

'Oh, some band. Can't really remember who. I just remember the words.'

Total porky. I knew all too well who wrote that. Vince Clarke (before he abandoned Depeche Mode), from the track 'Just Can't Get Enough'. The album: *Speak and Spell* (1981). Always hated the way people shouted out 'SEX' at the school disco whenever Dave Gahan sang 'I just can't get enough', but I guess Lisa would've been too young to know that.

'Well, I'll never forget them either,' she beamed. She kissed me again, briefly this time. We stood there for a moment, not knowing what to say, then she said quietly, 'Well, I suppose I should head home.'

'Of course,' I stammered, a little unsure of what to do. I dashed to the roadside and hailed a taxi for her. I waved to her as the car pulled away and she waved back. I stood there for a moment, watching as the taxi disappeared into the traffic, then headed up towards Christchurch and the warren of tiny streets beyond it, where Lisa was living with some people I hadn't met yet.

I stood there for a long time imagining her in the taxi thinking, I hoped, of me also. God, I really had impressed her. I could do no wrong it seemed. I was the king. Who would've thought? Couldn't wipe the grin off my face as I walked up George's Street past all the pretty people framed in the window of the Globe. I usually envied them. They always seemed so at ease and super-confident and always so interested in each other. But none of it mattered to me that night. I just kept walking and felt that I was just like them really. Maybe I didn't know what to say to a hairdresser to get a decent haircut, or still wore jeans instead of combats (or whatever they were wearing now), but I could be like them. I mean, Lisa was like them and she was with me now.

I stopped at the canal for a breather and sat down on a bench. I could see the swans with their heads tucked under their wings asleep in the rushes like pale ghosts oblivious, like me, to all the Saturday night madness going on around us. I took a cigarette out of the packet, lit up and thought about the night, reliving each line that Lisa had said to me, though I kept getting them muddled, which was surprising because I'm usually pretty good at remembering stuff. 'I'll never forget them, either.' Yes, that was it. I was about to go home when some young one in a *Daz*-white belly-top rushed straight past me and into the bushes, then puked.

The moment had been kinda ruined but I didn't mind. The swans didn't seem to notice either.

I put out my smoke, got up and asked her if she was okay. 'Grand yeah, thanks,' she said, still bent over double, then retched again. Suddenly, some bloke came running down the pathway out of nowhere, grabbed me by the shoulder and swung me round to face him.

'Are you trying to shift me bird, you little prick?' he fumed, his nose pushed up against mine.

Fuck sake, I didn't need to. Couldn't he see from my face that I had the contented look of someone who already had, and not the bothered look of someone, like him, who was still trying? And besides, he must have thought I was either desperate or as drunk as him to try to shift someone who had just, moments before, unceremoniously vomited in the bushes. Then again, maybe at this point the contentment I just mentioned had been replaced by fear.

The girl blurted out in a raspy voice behind us, 'Samo, it's cool. He just asked me if I was alright. Leave him alone for fuck's sake.'

I was pretty relieved that she'd intervened at that moment, because Samo seemed like he was looking for a fight one way or the other. He grabbed me again anyway and pulled me down into a head-lock which he held for what seemed like ages, then laughed and let me go. I stood there trying to catch my breath, as pale now as the girl.

'Fair play to ya. Just taking the piss, bud. Don't worry bout it. Too mucha dat bleedin vodka and Redbull. Can't hold her drink or what. That right, Samantha,' he said to the girl as she stood up and wiped her mouth, like he was trying to impress her. Or maybe me. I laughed a little back, more out of relief than anything else, and said in a trembling voice, 'No problem, Samo. I think she'll be alright. Night now.'

I started walking briskly away down the pathway towards the Portobello Bridge, and when I looked back Samo and the girl were snogging away there beside the sleeping swans. My legs were shaking a little, so I decided to avoid any more drunken encounters and went the long way home, up past the sleeping houses of Mount Pleasant Avenue, passing the occasional ol' fella stumbling home from a local pub, and finally onto Belgrave Square with its red-bricked Georgian houses and their tall, white-framed windows.

I was relieved when I opened the door of my flat and collapsed on the couch. I thought again about what had happened with Lisa and wondered if it had really happened at all. At least, the way I remembered it. Was it just some Saturday night snog, like Samo and his girl, or a real kiss? I wasn't quite sure .

I didn't put on any music, though, like I usually did, but just sat there slumped looking at a poster I had bought when I first moved into the flat and stuck up on the magnolia wall with bluetac. It was one by that Austrian fella Klimt, 'The Kiss'. I realised I hadn't noticed it for ages. It was just there, I suppose, like the dun-coloured couch with its golden tassels that I'd bought for a tenner in Oxfam; or the fold-up table by the window where I ate my breakfast.

But that night I saw the poster as if for the first time: the way the man leaned around towards the woman, and she nestled her head into his shoulder, her eyes closed. The moment just before they kissed. Or was it just after? Which got me wondering why it was called 'The Kiss', given that they weren't actually kissing. Still, I liked to think my kiss with Lisa was like that, though I was realistic about my abilities in that department. I also noticed just then that the poster was slightly crooked and wondered why I hadn't spotted that before.

Anyway, I guess my kiss with Lisa was the real thing alright. She called me again the next day and we arranged to go for a meal this time, which I took to be an encouraging sign.

Three weeks later, Lisa was kicked out of her flat for falling behind on the rent. Being a musician is a precarious lifestyle if you're on the wrong side of a record deal. I understood that very well, so I offered to let her stay at my place *for a while*. I don't think she heard the last three words in that offer, and I guess we ended up living together because she had become distracted at the end of a sentence. And, anyway, I was too in awe of her to point it out later when she arrived with all her stuff, including a potted plant for every available corner, table top, counter and shelf in an already overcrowded flat (actually bedsit is a more accurate term) as well as one of those inflatable, red couches that people were into lately, though personally I thought were pretty uncomfortable and kinda impractical if you were a smoker like Lisa. And me for that matter. Still, I didn't mind putting my old couch in the neighbour's skip. Those golden tassels really were terrible. As she pointed out, her stuff brightened up the place, and I had to agree. Out with the old and all that other stuff.

It was all a bit sudden, though, I have to admit. But I was kinda flattered too. And we had, after all, a common language: the power of music. That was the most important thing. I was feeling quite optimistic about the whole thing really, which surprised me.

# September (1:18)

I can't help it. I am what I am. A product of my environment, as they say, and my older brothers' taste in music in particular. I was too young to buy records, so I listened to what they listened to. (Though I'm jumping ahead of myself.) I'll just say I was an early developer when it came to experimental music, if nothing else.

It started one night over the rainbow-colour thing they put up on BBC 2 after the National Anthem. They were playing some track. I was eight. I liked it. No, I bloody well loved it. My parents were out visiting my granny at the time and my brothers were out getting drunk on Scrumpy Jack in a field somewhere in Finglas. I suppose I hadn't heard much music up to then, at least not that I can remember, but this was different. It just started with this melody that kept going round and round on a piano or something, and then some other instrument would come in with some other loop and that would go on for ages as well. It was like being on a merry-go-round that just kept getting slightly faster and faster as all the faces of the people watching become blurry and indistinct, until you forgot they were there altogether. Honestly, after a while it began to make me feel almost dizzy. Or maybe even hypnotized, and I don't mean that in some stupid metaphorical sense.

And then that bloke from the BBC would speak for a moment and the music would change as if they had heard him or something. It freaked me out. I didn't know they could do that and it kinda made me wonder if they could see me sitting there in the living room, my face pressed up against the telly. At that point it didn't matter because I was going round on that whirligig of music, layer upon layer of it, oblivious until suddenly I heard another voice shout, 'You'll ruin your bloody eyesight with your head stuck to the box like that'. For a minute I thought it was part of the track, but turned my head slightly to find my mother standing over me.

I suppose the moment had been kinda broken. I jumped up from the floor and tried to act as normal as possible, which in my case wasn't that normal anyway. I saw my oul' lad watching distrustfully from the frame of the door. I asked questions about my granny while straining to listen to the music in the background, but then the BBC bloke suddenly seemed to lose it completely and shouted out in a big, booming, demonic voice 'AAAAAGGHHHHH' and my mother nearly jumped out of her skin. The oul' lad walked over to the telly and pressed the big silver on/off button, and the music stopped with that popping sound tellies used to make, with the fluorescent dot lingering in the middle for a couple of seconds before disappearing.

And that was it. I heard the oul' fella mumbling as he left the room, 'Boy's not right in the head.' To make it up to them I offered to make me ma a cup of tea and bring it up to her in bed, in the vain hope that I could distract her for a bit longer and turn the telly back on. But she was having none of it and made me go to bed instead despite my protestations.

You know, now that I think about it, the whole experience has been quite like a lot of other experiences in my life that are too personal to mention in words, but suffice to say there's a big, long-drawn-out, ecstatic build-up and then the bloody telly's turned off just when... well I've said enough already. I think you know what I'm getting at.

Anyway, I needed to get that piece of music. It drove me mad, kept going round and round my little head like the crazy loops in that song. Over the following weeks I had to create a series of ridiculous ailments so that I could stay up in the faint hope that they would play it again. In any case, the ailment was real enough: I couldn't sleep with the excitement, so I wasn't totally lying to my parents, though maybe I went too far when I suggested I'd been food poisoned by my mother's cooking.

They never did play the track again, though. Eventually I came clean with me ma and I even got her to take me to some place called Platinum Discs to try and find a copy. It was a Saturday afternoon, four days before Christmas. Me ma was visibly uncomfortable as we stood there at the back of the enormous queue. I thought this was a good sign. I wasn't alone: other people had obviously heard that song too. When we eventually got to the counter a bloke stood there with that glazed over look people have who work in crap record shops. I hadn't recognised that look yet so I was still feeling optimistic.

Me ma stammered: 'He heard a piece of music... On the BBC would ya be mindin. Any chance you'd know what it was?'

I jumped in, excitedly: 'BBC 2. Just after midnight. Saturday, December 7$^{th}$. No singing.' I started to hum the main melody as best as I could remember it. It was a pretty good rendition, I thought. I really did believe he'd know it. He was a professional after all.

'No idea,' he said with a distinct lack of interest. 'Have you any idea how many pieces of music they play on telly these days?'

'A lot,' I said, which was true, jumping in again. 'But this was *good*.'

Me ma cut across me before I could start another rendition: 'I'm sorry, it's just he's driving me bleedin crazy hummin that damn tune all day long.'

Hello. I know I was only eight years old but I was actually in the room at the time.

'Is there anythin ya think he might like?' she pleaded. It really was a plea from the heart. I hadn't realised until then that love wasn't the reason we were in the shop in the first place.

Left that stupid Platinum Discs with a copy of 'Walking in the Air' and I've never been back since. Even then I knew a good cover from a bad cover and this one was shite. I mean, what was with all those snowmen? It made sense when I heard the bloody song, if you could call it that. In fact, I'd heard it about a million times already on UTV. I fucking hated it. And there was bloody singing on it.

To keep the peace I had to play it all Christmas, but once the silly season was over I ritually burned it in the fireplace, which caused a bit of a mess and a pretty bad smell that stayed in the house for weeks. I didn't know at that point that vinyl was a polymer that, if burned, produced a slightly noxious gas that could cause vomiting and nausea. How could I know? There was nothing on the sleeve about not burning the stupid thing.

My mother wasn't impressed. Just as well I'd waited till after Christmas or I suspect that Santa might have turned out to have been Presbyterian that year. In any case, I really didn't want another Action Man. Then again, with four of them, you had about the right number to start a band. Spent months searching through catalogues to see if you could buy instruments for them instead of tanks and guns, but I had no luck, and my mother refused point blank to ring the manufacturers to see if they would be interested in making them. You *could* get a pink guitar for Barbie though, but I knew I would get beaten up on the street if anyone saw it. And besides, I was really after keyboards and drum machines even then, so I just made some from cardboard, Airfix paint and some double-sided Sellotape.

Took me another eight years to discover what that bloody record was, but that's a long story and I'll spare you the details. In any case, I was a little disappointed to find out in the end that it was by Mike Oldfield, though I will say *Tubular Bells* was his finest piece of work. Anyway, I'd moved on to other musical pastures by then and really just wanted to know for sentimental reasons.

*

I'd been living with Lisa for over two months. It was hard sometimes, but we still appeared to have a common ground on the music front. I suppose the honeymoon period was over as they say, but then that just meant we were really getting to know each other. I realised that, as well as being intelligent and funny, she could also be, well, a bit moody. But then, who isn't? This was the real thing. Loving the whole person and all that stuff. I'd read that in a book Lisa had given me. (*The Whole Person* I think it was called, though most of them were getting jumbled up in my head by this point.)

Anyway, I'd been playing the track 'Let the Happiness In' by David Sylvian (former front man of Japan – icon, cult figure, and now recluse) from his album *Secrets of the Beehive* (1987). Lisa hated it. The whole album really, but that track in particular. It was mid-September and, for some reason, I always felt the need to play the song when the days started to get short again. I think it may also have been because the opening track – coming in at a stunning one minute eighteen seconds – was called, well, 'September'. I should add also that the word 'happiness' in the title of 'Let The Happiness In' is a tad misleading. The key word is 'in'.

Lisa, I was discovering, wasn't into the whole New Romantic thing and, in particular, songs by former New Romantic artists who had discovered jazz and wrote introspective ballads about looking at seagulls. The track was really about loneliness, but Lisa could never see the connection despite my best efforts. That was another reason why I kept playing the track. I figured she'd get it eventually.

'Will you stop playing that fucking song? It's thirty years old for Christ sake,' she said, a little irritated, one Saturday afternoon as she sat on the inflatable couch putting a new string on her guitar. (Well, Saturday 20th September at about 4.30pm to be precise. I'm good on dates. Never forget birthdays or anniversaries, which always makes my mother proud and seems to impress girls, at least for a couple of weeks.)

'Not quite. Recorded in spring 1987 at Chateau Miraval, Le Val …'

'My point exactly. The fucking song is nearly thirty years old,' she said, her eyes darting up from the guitar. She never was strong on arithmetic, Lisa. But then, she was artistic so you could understand that failing.

'So!' I said, maybe getting a little defensive. 'A classic album is a classic precisely because it doesn't date. It gets better with time like a good…'

'Wine. Yadda, yadda, yadda. If it was really a classic song I would've heard about it before I met you.'

She was getting very personal indeed. I had thought I could turn her around on this one, if nothing else. It really was a classic album. The fact that very few other people realised that yet was neither here nor there. Anyway, I was losing the battle, and I guess I decided to get personal back.

'Well, fuckin Elvis has been dead for *nearly* fifty years. And as far I can remember he died on the bog wearing a silver suit, with a fuckin treble cheeseburger in his available hand.'

Uh. I'd gone too far. I knew it. The red mist was about to descend.

'Don't ever disrespect The King like that again in my presence,' she said, almost inaudibly. She kept tightening the string and I could hear it creaking in a funny way. I didn't know much about guitars, but I knew that string was about to snap. The signs were looking bad.

There was a long silence which I hadn't intended to be the first to break. *Say nothing, say nothing, say nothing,* I repeated over and over in my head. But then the bloody string gave way with a twang, and I guess my willpower snapped with it, because I blurted out like a child trying to win the 'quiet game' in school after drinking an entire bottle of soda stream: 'He didn't even write his own songs for god sakes!'

I stood there waiting for the backlash.

'No, you're right. He didn't,' she said calmly, seeming to concede at least that much. Huh, she was finally coming to see my point. I felt a moral victory coming on.

'He actually *employed* people who *could* write songs instead of writing terrible ones himself. Now turn the fucking thing off before I do it myself and throw the CD in the fucking microwave.'

Fooled again. Lisa did have a good sense of timing that I didn't share, which explains why I wasn't very good at playing music (and why she had taken to drying her clothes on my Yamaha PSR-S550). She threw the guitar down on the floor and leaned back into the couch and crossed her arms.

'Honey,' I said, 'you know that song is very special for me, especially at this time of...'

'Yeah, when your last girlfriend left you. I know,' she said bluntly.

'That was only part of it,' I sulked.

'Get over it, Tom.'

Had I mentioned that? My name? Well, I guess Lisa has just done it for me. I would rather have told you myself because it seemed lately that whenever she said it, it had become a substitute for asshole. Still, a name's a name and I suppose I could've left out the context. But you see where we were at already. The *whole person* shit was beginning to seem like a recipe for keeping people locked in unhappy relationships.

Anyway I found that I couldn't call Lisa by her name anymore after that conversation, so I just started calling her Honey. And after several similar arguments that day it became furthered shortened to Hon. All the sweetness after all, as my mother says, is in the last two letters.

Next day when I came home there was a big wall-hanging of Elvis over our bed. I have to admit it kind of creeped me out. It was one of those kitsch things. Like those wall hangings of Jesus you see in Brazil that looked liked they'd been designed by a Christian with a very liberal view regarding hallucinogenic inspiration. I really wasn't that keen on the idea of another man watching over us like that as we made love either. Then again, that hadn't happened in a while – I mean the love-making thing, not being watched, which only happened once and that was by accident – but, if we had, it might have affected my performance: that big fake, smiley Elvis looking down on me like *he* was Jesus Christ or something. Lisa obviously thought he was, that much was clear. When one human being refers to another human being as *the* King you know there's something else going on. Not even Henry VIII called himself *the* King and he wasn't a man known for his humility from what I'd heard on the *History Channel*.

I was standing there looking at Elvis looking back at me when Lisa came in.

'Hi,' I mumbled. 'I see you got a new...'

'You like it,' she said, and I don't think it was a question.

'Yeah. It's cool.'

Lisa came up beside me and looked up at it with me as if we were in an art gallery.

'Yeah,' I continued, feeling I had to say something, 'very... vibrant... colours.'

It was the best I could do under the circumstances. I could see it wasn't the response she expected.

# Girlfriend in a Coma (2:03)

I should say at this point that I have two older brothers. Maybe I said that already. Doesn't matter. In the absence of *Tubular Bells* it was a straight choice between the joys of experimentation in synthesizer technology and the hippy, drippy ballads of Chris de Burgh, who was a favourite of my older, older brother. Actually, it was his entire record collection though, in fairness to him, I think he only bought the records to impress his girlfriend. It worked. They played 'Satin Green Shutters' at their wedding. I almost died with embarrassment. As did my brother. Then again, maybe he was just nervous. Weddings are hard I've heard and sometimes love asks a lot of a man as I was about to discover in the coming weeks. They looked happy, though, as they walked up the aisle after the ceremony, all smiles and flowers and flashing cameras as 'Don't Pay the Ferryman' boomed in the background.

God, it *was* hard living with another person, though. I mean, you just can't be that charming all the time, and I hadn't much practice at it over periods of more than two hours. Well, I had no practice with it whatsoever to be perfectly frank. There's the whole toilet seat thing which I thought was a myth but is actually true. (She thought I was becoming more considerate, but I just started to piss with the seat down and kinda hoped I missed it but I never did.) Then there's the 'I want my space' buzz, which means I'd have to go for a long walk around Ranelagh or even Donnybrook in the cold and rain, shuffling through the litter of fallen leaves that were piled on the pavements, when I'd rather be in watching the telly or something. Oh yeah, and there's the telly itself. 'I want to watch this; you want to watch that' saga. Not to mention her annoying habit of snoring in her sleep, which she categorically denied. I mean, how could she know if she snores in her sleep or not? It's a, it's a... what you call it... oxymoron or something. Her answer to the riddle: 'Because none of my previous boyfriends ever mentioned it.' Shit, how many of them were there and why were they too scared to say it?

Anyway, I don't think having two brothers prepares you for the whole co-habitation experience. They had problems too, I noticed, living with other people (and they both had more than one room to live in through the whole ordeal).

Maybe if Lisa and me had two rooms we could at least have a hi-fi in both so that we could have a nice evening together, then go listen to our music separately and sort out the mother of all household compromises. I couldn't understand how I was the one who ended up having to use an iPod in my own home, which pissed me off because I preferred the ambience of a room (particularly this room, which is why I took the flat in the first place) to headphones. It was, after all, my flat first and I felt I should be able to play my own music at my own time of choosing.

I guess you may have noticed that I'm kinda particular about my music. But then, so was Lisa. I respected that. Music is important. It says a lot about a person. I just didn't see why it was me who'd ended up wearing the headphones in the homestead, that's all.

Besides, it's not as if Lisa was exactly into modern music herself. I mean, she liked Johnny Cash, Gene Pitney, Elvis (as I mentioned earlier I think), and some blokes from New York called Anaesthetica. (And from what I could tell those Anaesthetica fellas were definitely using more than prescription medications, though I did like the way they used the bass as a lead instrument.) Also that whole alt-country thing, whatever that means, which was a recent enthusiasm.

Country? Yeah, that was good. I could work with that. I knew a great joke about country which I was pretty sure I hadn't told her before. It was a wet Wednesday in October. Approximately 5.45. I know this because I'd just come back from another poxy shift in that dump that pretended to be a video shop, and where I'd become the bloke with the glazed over look on his face. I was also soaked right through because I'd forgotten to take an umbrella and had no money for a taxi.

'Lisa!' I said, trying to raise my spirits as I took off my sodden jacket.

'Yeah,' she replied, without looking up from the magazine she was reading.

'What happens when you play a country and western song backwards?'

'You hear the devil singing "Let the Happiness In",' she said without a moment's hesitation. Then, glancing up, 'On an electric guitar.'

No. Goddamn it. My punch line was better than that. (And it hurt. She bloody well knew how much that song meant to me.)

'Very funny. No, seriously?' I bounced back, as I dripped a pool of water onto the floor about my feet.

She stood up, ignoring me, and began to remove some dried up leaves from her plants, the rain splattering against the window in big, fat drops. (They were most definitely her plants. I wasn't even allowed to touch them, which was bloody hard because they were all over the place. They came with her and I was beginning to suspect that, when she left, they would leave with her also.)

Anyway, my attempt to lighten the atmosphere wasn't going well and by now my jeans were stuck to my legs. I was starting to feel the pressure. And there's no worse time to lose your confidence than in the middle of a joke. (Or I suppose while playing a classic track live and forgetting the lyrics.)

'Well,' I pressed on, 'Hank gets a new pick-up truck, his dog comes home, and he leaves... Shit, no, that's not right. Wait a sec... Oh yeah: he gets... *Hank* gets a new pick-up truck, his dog comes home, and he remarries his estranged ex-wife.'

Lead balloon, people, lead balloon. She used to laugh at all my jokes. Now she fondled her plants, and they don't even talk or respond emotionally. I could've handled her having a relationship with a cat, but plants seemed like an insult, to say the least.

'Right. I get it,' she said flatly. 'Country music is more depressing than that crap you listen to, and everyone who plays it is called Wank.'

The respect had gone. I guess her taste in music was maybe something not to joke about. I'd also noticed that she was playing 'Girlfriend in a Coma' a lot lately and she didn't even like The Smiths.

I went to the bathroom to get a towel and dry myself off, while Lisa fondled the cheese plant by the window.

# Hurt (3:38)

'You're living in the past, Tom,' she said so often it had become like a skip on a record that I was getting pretty fed up listening to. She had also started to pin it up in the bathroom as a kind of negative affirmation, just in case she managed to get through a day without mentioning it herself. She was at it again, and I wasn't even playing one of my records but instead found myself on that bouncy castle pretending to be a sofa, listening to Emmylou Harris of all people. This time I decided not to pretend I hadn't heard her.

'No. That's not fair. I'm just living in a different bit of the past than you,' I said.

'Maybe. Just happens to be the most embarrassing five years in the history of mankind. Ever. Circa 1979 to1983,' she said, as though she were an authority on the matter, which was presumptuous given that she was a zygote at the beginning of 1979 and was a long way from using words like *circa* by 1983. Then again, maybe not. She did go to the John Scottus Eriugena School for exceptionally right-on parents in Donnybrook. I may have just gone to the local Christian Brothers but I knew my specialist subject and I wasn't letting it go this time.

'That's just not fair,' I said finally. 'I mean, I can accept that the whole exploration of the make-up thing was a mistake, but those people were pioneers. Pioneers,' I repeated emphatically. 'And besides, I think, really, the late medieval period was pretty bad.'

'I meant musically,' she snapped back.

'So did I,' I retaliated. 'I fucking hate those madrigals with all that hey nonny nonny crap.' (They'd played a lot of that stuff on BBC 2 during those weeks when I was trying to find *Tubular Bells*.)

'Right. Worse than say... Let's see: "Here in my car/ I feel safest of all/ I can lock all my doors/ It's the only way to live"' Pause. '"In cars."'

She knew she had me on the ropes with that one and I could see a faint, self-satisfied smile forming on her lips.

'That was inspired by the writings of J G Ballard,' I retorted. 'It's one of the great lyrics about urban alienation.'

'Case closed,' she said and I could see that she meant it.

But there was no closing the case. At least I tried to appreciate her music. I was really quite getting to like that Johnny Cash fella. His rendition of Depeche Mode's 'Personal Jesus' was pretty good. (Would've preferred if he tried a more seminal track like 'Black Celebration' from the 1986 album of the same title, but it was a move in the right direction, in my opinion.) And that song 'Hurt'. Wow! Even made me cry when I saw the video with Lisa one night on some music show we were watching on MTV – the kind of event that usually ended up in us reopening the fracture over the whole divergent taste in music thing and me sleeping on the floor. But 'Hurt'. That really was a powerful track and responsible for one of the truly touching moments in our relationship. That is, until I pointed out that 'Hurt' was a pretty depressing song in a great tradition of depressing songs, not unlike 'Love Will Tear Us Apart' by Joy Division or...

'Fuck off,' she said, as she got off the couch in a huff and went into the toilet so she could have the drama of slamming a door. (One of the great difficulties of living in a bedsit is there's nowhere to go when you have a fight, or doors to slam for that matter.) Unfortunately, she had to come out a few minutes later because it's pretty cold in there even in November which, I guess, added to the indignity of the whole situation from her point of view.

'You're sleeping in the spare room,' she said bluntly as she walked past me towards the bed. She hadn't even given me a chance to make a qualified apology. The fact that it was coming up to Johnny Cash's anniversary probably also contributed to her mood. But then I was upset too. I really was growing to like the man's work, and as far as I'm aware he never stooped so low as to play Vegas in a silver suit.

'Hon, we don't have a spare room.'

'Well then, I guess you're sleeping on the street.'

I thought she was joking but she meant it all right. I had to knock over to my mate Gary in Phibsboro, who was a keyboardist with a Depeche Mode tribute band as well as being a roadie which, I suppose, paid the bills.

Have I mentioned Gary already? Maybe not. He was the one with the endless supply of grass and he discovered somehow that Lisa liked 'The Model' by Kraftwerk. I'm jumping ahead, though. The grass and Kraftwerk were to come into play later, during a last ditch attempt on my part at some form of reconciliation between us. I guess you know already that she ended up at the airport with someone else, so I'm not giving anything away when I say it could've gone better.

# Autobahn (22:47)

Okay. So what did happen next? Shit, I know there was something else. Can't remember it now, sorry. Grass can do that to your train of thought. Suppose I'll just do away with the suspense and cut straight to what I had billed as 'Autobahn Night with Lisa & Tom'. I thought putting her name first was a nice gesture. It summed up the whole sense of meeting each other half way which I liked and was to be the theme of the night, I hoped, in more ways than one.

Lisa had also been feeling guilty lately. I think maybe it was about threatening to short-circuit my *Secrets of the Beehive* CD (which was an original edition and possibly the first copy purchased in this country). And maybe also about the Elvis wall-hanging, though she still hadn't taken it down. And maybe even about making me listen to my music on headphones which had, I have to admit, made things a bit better on the domestic level, so maybe she was right on that one, though I still resented it.

I'd also apologised about the Johnny Cash night and went out and bought her the complete box-set, as well as a special edition of the single 'Hurt', which had the video on it.

To my complete surprise she agreed – though for one night, and one night only – to let me be the DJ in the household. Love certainly was hard. But compromise was a beautiful thing, and I suddenly understood why my brother had allowed 'Satin Green Shutters' to be played on the most important day of his life. At least, it had been the most important day of his life until the day of his divorce. Don't recall there being any music that day, but that's another story. Anyway, I'm digressing. Back to Autobahn Night.

'Okay, Hon, I'm all yours,' Lisa said as she returned from rehearsal, putting her guitar case down in the middle of the floor. She was looking great. Hair in braids, dark blue eye-shadow, a black dress I really liked. She certainly was making the effort. I'd already forgiven her for being three hours and twenty-two minutes late.

I had a bottle of wine open, mood lighting (she'd taught me all about that), candles, the whole thing going on. Oh yeah, and five perfectly rolled joints made with the finest grass money can buy in a country where you have to accept that there's probably oregano and arsenic mixed in with it to give it some extra bulk.

Lisa seemed genuinely surprised at the effort I'd put into the whole evening and even made a point of coming over to kiss me, though I had the feeling that it was more of a symbolic kiss than a real one. But hey, it was a promising start. All going to plan, though the mood lighting made Elvis look even creepier than usual and I was worried that he might, at some point, play into my paranoid tendencies. Shit. He was already playing on my paranoid tendencies or else I wouldn't even have had that thought in the first place. And I hadn't even puffed the Magic Dragon yet.

I tried to put Elvis out of my head as I took her coat and hung it on the door. We relaxed for a while on the sofa and I asked her about *her band's* music. (I was becoming suspicious about whether or not they even existed because they never seemed to play any gigs, and she was uncharacteristically vague about what they'd been rehearsing lately.)

'Oh, you know, Hon, just some ideas,' she said, off-handedly.

84

'Country stuff?' I quizzed.

'Oh, different stuff. Don't really want to talk about it.'

I let it go, and after a while we smoked the peace pipe (or maybe two) and I insisted that we lie down on the floor so that we could get more relaxed.

'Oh, for Christ sakes Hon, I'll crease my dress,' Lisa said, trying to disguise her impatience.

'Don't worry. It'll be worth it. I promise,' I said, trying to keep the mood right for what was to follow.

I don't think Lisa fully understood that *Autobahn* was an album you had to fully let yourself go to appreciate, but I was optimistic that she'd get it. (That's why I'd got the finest grass available in the first place, in the hope that she mightn't notice that it was 22 minutes and 17 seconds long. And that was just side one. Personally, I think side two is better though we never got that far. But I'm zooming ahead again.)

Anyway, I talked her into lying down beside me, after I put down a couple of blankets to help us get comfortable on the wooden floor. I waited till Lisa seemed chilled, then jumped up and put the stylus down onto the record. I looked at her lying there as the track began with the slight hiss and crackle of an old record, and realised why I had gone to all the bother. She just looked so... I dunno, at peace I suppose. I hadn't seen her with that expression on her face in such a long time. I lay back down beside her and closed my eyes as the track built up slowly, keyboard layer by keyboard layer.

I actually thought it was going quite well. I was definitely in the zone as the vocals kicked in after the long intro. You had to give Kraftwerk that. They were the masters of minimalism in their red shirts, black trousers and little robot faces. I was having a pretty good visualisation by now of driving down a straight, infinitely long, empty Autobahn at high speed, when there was a sudden flash of lightening. Interesting, I thought to myself. I hadn't expected that. It didn't even coincide with the escalation of the bass keyboard line.

'Tom, you are such an asshole,' Lisa's voice rasped just inches above my face, which gave me a terrible shock. She'd switched on the bloody light and, I'd just realised, used the words 'Tom' and 'Asshole' in the same sentence. I looked up at her, dazed.

'Have you noticed, Tom,' she asked calmly, 'that Japan rhymes with Duran...' (perfectly timed pause) 'Duran?'

'Jesus, Lisa,' I said in a somewhat distant voice that only vaguely resembled my own. 'Which came first the... the... the... the fuckin zebra or the crossing? Duran Duran were just a bunch of tarts in it for the cash and the birds. I can't believe you'd even mention them in the same breath.'

It didn't matter. She was already putting on her coat as I stumbled into a standing position and immediately got a head-rush. I had to sit back down before I could say another word. This time Lisa had the pleasure of slamming both the door of our flat and the hall door outside, waking all the neighbours in the process.

And then to complicate matters there was more banging on the door. I thought, for a moment, that Lisa might have had a change of heart, but unfortunately that wasn't the case. It was Eithne from upstairs, wagging her finger at me while Kraftwerk played on in the background. I can safely say that there's nothing worse than trying to placate a middle-aged woman in pink slippers and matching dressing-gown when you're off your trolley and the word Elvis keeps coming into the conversation. Anyway, I eventually convinced Eithne *not* to phone the landlord, but only after I'd promised to do her grocery shopping for a month and not to play music after eleven.

I must admit I was in shock. First with Lisa storming off and then the whole hassle with Eithne. Lisa had definitely crossed a line this time. I was going to buy the poster of the cover of *Quiet Life* from eBay and put it beside Elvis to get her back. I sat there for the rest of the evening in silence, elaborating on the plan. The more I thought about it though (which was a lot) I had to admit that Japan's image – if not the music – had dated somewhat. And the idea of two good-looking men (had to give Elvis that much) looking over us, in the unlikely event that we ever made love again, was just two damn intimidating to contemplate.

I decided to drop the idea.

Didn't matter anyway, as things turned out. Lisa came over the next day when I was at work and picked up her stuff. I know I hated that red sofa but the place did look suddenly strange without it. And without the plants; and the checkered blue tablecloth; and the lava lamp; and the guitar; and all the leads that were usually lying about the place. I was still too numb to really feel Lisa's absence, but all the stuff that had just disappeared somehow made the place feel empty and lonely.

When I went to the bathroom to wash my face I noticed the mirror was gone too. But she'd forgotten one of the postcards she liked to pin up around the place. It was one of those 1950s posters of a small boy sitting on the floor, listening to a record player, and a slightly older girl dancing beside him. The caption across the top read, in jagged letters: 'ROCK & ROLL'. And beneath it, in smaller writing: 'Hey Daddio, the devil's got another one of our children.'

Now that I think about it, maybe Lisa had left that there deliberately, but that didn't matter. I sat on the linoleum floor and looked at it like it was maybe a goodbye note, or even a love letter she'd never written. It was then that I realised she was gone for good, and I suddenly missed her and wondered if she missed me too. I think I knew the answer to that question but, for then at least, I pretended that she might have second thoughts and come back. I guess the truth was that we'd brought the worst out in each other.

*

A couple of weeks later, though, Gary told me that Lisa had met some other bloke. Musician apparently. I might be reading between the lines here but I got the impression that she'd maybe met him *before* she moved out. Which meant that... Sweet mother of Elvis! I looked across the room at our  – okay *my* – bed. They had (oh no, oh no)... They'd been... in my... while I...

No no no no no no nO NO. I decided that I wasn't going to go down that route in my head. Jealousy is a terrible thing. Even I know that. Eats the heart away and all that other stuff it does to you that I can't quite remember, but it's all bad. Read that somewhere or maybe it was in a song lyric. May even have been Johnny Cash. (In fairness, he was a damn fine lyricist, the more I thought about it, and he did say interesting stuff in his songs.) No. I wasn't going down that route. *Green was as bad as red. Green was as bad as red. Green was as bad as red...* But then again.

I decided to meet Gary for a pint to see if he had any other information. I was sitting in the snug in Slattery's drinking a hot port, waiting for him to arrive. In the background I could hear the trad musicians starting up a tune. The barman leaned over from the hatch.

'Another port, then?' he asked, his podgy face a little red as he wiped the sweat from his forehead.

'No, I'm grand thanks.' I pointed to the half-full glass. In fairness, I'd been sitting with it for at least an hour and I think the barman was getting impatient with my drinking in moderation tactic – otherwise known in the bar trade as the punter staying in out of the cold. Thankfully, at that moment, Gary pulled open the small door to the snug.

Funny thing with Gary. Even people who don't know him act like his best friend. He has that quality. He looked straight over to the barman: 'How's it going?'

'Not too bad, and yourself?' said the barman, cheerfully.

'Yeah, good. Really good,' he said, like he really meant it.

'What can I get ya?'

'Eh, a pint of Guinness and whatever this *retro-bate* is having,' he said, making his usual private joke about me.

'Nothing apparently,' the barman said flatly.

'Actually, I may as well have another port,' I piped in.

'Fair enough,' the barman said, looking at me with that barman look, then smiling at Gary before disappearing from the hatch.

'Hey man, how are you?' Gary asked, turning to me for the first time as he sat down.

'Well, okay. I mean under the…'

'Yeah, yeah, I know. Shit isn't it?' he said, with a concerned note in his voice. 'But all's not lost.'

'What?'

'Nothing. Just a figure of speech, Tom. You've got your health and your looks. The future is painted red. Am I right?' He laughed.

'I'm not so sure, Gary. Yunno, it's been kinda rough,' I said with a little self-pity.

He turned and looked at me for a moment. 'She got ya bad. But fuck her. I mean, I liked the girl, but it's not worth all this heartache.'

'Maybe,' I mused.

'Listen, I already told ya. She's moved on. It's over. No point wasting your, yunno, vital energies thinking about it.'

I sat in silence wasting some more vital energy thinking about it. Gary has some crazy theory that we're born with a certain amount of energy, like a charged battery or something, and if we use it on bad stuff then there's none left for the good stuff. Which would explain his relentless optimism

'Look, listen to me.' He took me by the shoulders. 'Are you listening to me?'

'Yeah,' I replied, knowing I was about to get some of Gary's words of wisdom.

'I heard from someone, doesn't matter who, that she is leaving the fuckin country. She's going to New York. Outta here. So it's time…'

'When's she going?' I pounced.

'Lunchtime, Sunday before Christmas,' Gary said, before he could stop himself. 'But that's neither here nor there,' he continued, trying to cover his tracks, 'because you're moving on with your life. Right? Moving forward. Into the future.'

'Of course,' I said, off-handedly.

'Cool. That's settled. Yeah?'

'Absolutely. Got to save my vital energies, as you say.'

'You bet. Because guess what?' he added with thinly disguised excitement.

'What?'

'You're going to need it, my friend. Biggest gig yet.'

'No way,' I said, surprised.

'Yes way. The Sugar Club. New Year's Eve. *Da-Mode* will be bringing you, and other like-minded individuals, into the future with a sensational concert. Previously unheard back catalogue material. Visuals. The works. Couple of really cool DJs before and after us, but we're on for the big moment when the clock turns.'

'Seriously?'

'Yes, my friend. And, for your loyalty and support, one pair of tickets for your good self. Bring someone along. Someone new,' he said, as he handed me two yellow tickets.

'Excellent. I'll be there,' I said as I took them.

'I know you will. Always are. But the big question is, who'll be with you?'

'Oh, don't know. I'll find someone,' I said, getting caught up in Gary's enthusiasm. 'I dunno, maybe from the video shop.'

'As long as they respect the music, they're more than welcome.'

The barman appeared in the hatch again with the pint and the port. Gary paid for the drinks, then asked, 'Alright if I put a couple of posters up?'

'No problem. Sure, leave them with me,' the barman offered. Gary pulled a couple of rolled-up posters from his bag and handed them over to the barman. 'Much obliged, sir.'

The barman unrolled the poster. It was the usual cover band thing, with an actual picture of Depeche Mode on it, and, blazoned across the top: 'Black Celebration – A Night with Da-Mode – the ultimate Depeche Mode tribute band'.

'Modern music is it?' the barman asked, a little perplexed.

'You could say that.'

'Okay, sure I'll put them up anyway,' he said and disappeared again.

'Well, that should keep the tourists away,' I said, looking at Gary.

'Yeah. This one's for the real fans,' He took a large gulp from his pint. 'Big time.'

Still, as I walked home later, I found my mind constantly losing sight of the big gig and coming back to the fact that Lisa was not only seeing someone else but leaving the country as well. I mean, was I that bad? I tried to put it out of my mind, I really did, but it just wouldn't go away. I was also beginning to wonder how Gary knew all this in the first place, but since he was the only real mate I had I decided I'd let it go for the time being.

Lisa had been a bit obsessed before she left with those Anaesthetica fellas, and I had a feeling that she was maybe hoping to go to New York to give them a demo tape. (Who else would she give one to anyway, given that everyone else she liked was dead – and the way Anaesthetica were going, they'd be on the old Rock & Roll funeral pyre fairly soon if they didn't straighten up their lifestyle.) Yeah, that must've been it. They were probably playing a big gig as well, over the Christmas period, and she was going to meet them.

# Let the Happiness In (5:37)

Did I mention earlier that I wasn't at the airport? Okay, I was lying. I just wanted to appear more dignified than I am. I've already said too much. You know what I'm like by now. Even *I* know what I'm like by now. I just couldn't help myself. Had to see it with my own eyes. Slow down the car. Ease to a gentle stop. Pull down the window. Ask in a hushed, solemn tone: 'Guard, is there anything I can do? No? You're sure? Sir, any fatalities?'

If only I'd been so circumspect, though I'm jumping ahead again. Anyway, I don't even have a car, which is another reason why Lisa was so fond of quoting Gary Numan back at me. I had to take the bloody bus in the end because there were no taxis to be found anywhere in the city. 16A all the way, everyone else weighed down by rucksacks and tartan luggage cases, either going home from a wonderful winter break or about to start one.

I noticed a young woman in the seat in front of me with headphones on and realised it was probably a good way of avoiding conversation with so many people piling onto the bus. (I knew I needed to stay calm or I would probably do something stupid. I just wanted to see Lisa's new bloke with my own eyes. That's all. I swear.) Pretty sure you know by now what track I was rummaging for, even though it was well into December and I usually played *Tubular Bells* at this time of year to get back to my roots kinda thing.

I was still frantically fumbling in my bag when a middle-aged American tourist stood towering over me in the aisle. I knew he was American. He had green trousers on. I tried not to catch his eye and pretended to look out the window instead.

'Son? This seat free?' he boomed.

I turned my head slowly, caught his eye, nodded. (Why was it that when I was under pressure, I did the exact opposite of what I'd planned to do?) I still thought, though, that I had a chance to get the headphones on and avoid any further interaction if I could just keep my head together.

'Excellent. Going home, son?' he asked as he sat down beside me, squeezing me against the side of the bus, my face only inches from the fogged-over glass of the window.

'No, sir. I'm from here,' I said, forcing a smile.

'Ah, great. Going on vacation, then?'

'Yes. No. Not really. Just thought I'd like to… take a bus trip.'

'Whatever you're into son. Can see why you'd do it. Wonderful country you have here. Really wonderful. Even cities looks good over here. I'm from New York myself. You know, I just love the way you can see the sky the whole time. Wonderful.'

I nodded. He may not have realised it yet, but we were just about to enter one of the ugliest places in Ireland (and it was also raining which made it even uglier), that place being the first and last place everyone sees when they come to this wonderful country: Dublin International Airport. Not that I cared. Kinda suited my mood, now that I think about it.

'Just look at it would ya,' he said, looking past me. 'Wonderful.'

I turned my head to follow his gaze, but you couldn't see a damn thing with all the condensation on the window, except maybe a vague impression of a housing estate lurking beyond it. And if there was a skyline it was, I'm pretty sure, just a blank wall of grey.

94

'My people were from here. You probably guessed that,' he said with some pride. 'The green pants are a bit of a giveaway, but I'm not ashamed of my roots. No sir.'

I had to say something. It would've been rude not to.

'From Glasnevin?' I ventured. It was the first thing that came into my head, as usual, and we'd just passed Glasnevin cemetery from what I could see through the misted windows, so it was as good a name as any.

'Where's that, son? Mayo?' he asked, as though he'd actually heard of the place.

'Yes sir, I think so.'

We sat for a moment in silence, lines forming on his forehead beneath his big fop of silver hair.

'No,' he reflected. 'My people are the O'Briens of County Clare. Built that bridge over there. My great-great-uncle Jack O'Brien come over in the 60s. 1860s that is.' He looked at me and flashed a smile: 'Great Uncle Jack wasn't some peacenik hippy layabout, son. No sir. Hard working man. Like myself and all those before me.'

Funny that. My mother always said my great-great-great-grandfather built that bridge. In fact we'd gone to Clare on a family holiday specifically to see it. I was a bit disappointed at the time, and I made the mistake of saying that out loud. It's just I'd expected something like the Golden Gate, although I suppose for its time and place it was probably quite big but... Holy shit! It had just struck me. If his great-great-uncle was... Oh, dear God no. I was related to the man in the green trousers.

I thought it might be better to withhold that piece of the puzzle for the time being, given my current state of mind. I felt guilty though. Surely it would've been a pretty big deal for him to meet an actual blood relative who was actually Irish. Genes are thicker than water and all that, especially someone from, you know, the mothership or what have you. I just wasn't in the mood, given what I was about *not* to do. (Anyway, I would end up making it up to him later, so there's no need to feel guilty on my behalf.)

'Sounds like an interesting man,' I said, finally, hoping he would spare me the family genealogy, which I already knew in mind numbing detail; at least, on our side, but they're all the bloody same when it comes down to it. Such and such, lived there, died on such a date after a life of terrible hardship, had a child with the same name, who lived somewhere else then died from cholera at the age of...

'Oh, he was. Wonderful guy. I'm actually a Jack O'Brien myself. And my son, who's about your age son, is another Jack O'Brien. Junior in his case. I used to be called Jack O'Brien Jnr, but when my father passed away, Lord bless his soul, I figured I was Jack O'Brien Snr now. And my son could hardly be called Jack O'Brien Jnr Jnr could he!'

Always wondered about that. Jack now flashed another big smile at me. I have to say, for a man of his age he had a perfect set of teeth. His face then turned suddenly serious again and he said with visible emotion, 'Have to carry the flag. Roots. Very important things. Like the Oak Tree.'

'Wow,' I replied, trying to sound enthusiastic and use a lingo that he was comfortable with. It's important to make tourists welcome, given how the hospitality trade was suffering lately. And he was, after all, also a relative.

'Well, son, how about you? What do you do with yourself?' he asked with what sounded like genuine interest.

'Well sir, I'm between careers at the moment but I hope to work in the music industry at some point,' I said, as though I meant it, though it was just a bluff really. I suppose I just didn't want to disappoint him.

'Jeez. I may be able to help you there. I have a little distribution company on the side myself. Construction's my main business. Bridges actually. Big ones. Runs in the family. But I sure love my music. I intend to import traditional Irish music into the States. Export traditional American country into Ireland. You might call it a cultural exchange. I need someone on this end of the operation. You like country music son?' he asked, as he fixed me with his steely grey eyes.

'Very much, sir. Very much,' I said, as convincingly as possible. A break's a break, though I wasn't in the best mood to think about it right then.

Jack seemed to wait for me to say something else. I thought, given how much he liked to talk, it was an odd moment to throw the microphone in my direction. I felt suddenly under pressure to speak.

'Have you heard the joke about what happens when you play a country and western song backwards,' I asked, before I could stop myself, 'sir?'

The airport was jammers when I got there. Explains, I guess, why there were no taxis to be found in the whole of Dublin. They were all here in Dublin Airport, beeping their horns and getting in each other's way. I pushed a path through the crowds of people hauling heavy bags of luggage behind them in a seemingly random ritual of self-inflicted holiday-related stress.

I finally made my way into the entrance, then made a dash for the escalator, dodging past elderly tourists and bouncing off some backpacker's rucksack along the way. It was a relief to actually be on the thing. There was a momentary respite before I'd have to start the whole process again to get to the arrivals/departures area.

As we glided upwards I looked down on all the people. It was a weird sight. Reminded me of pictures I'd seen of Tokyo on telly. Seemed like a bad way to start your Christmas, in my opinion, everyone either dazed or bickering or in a state of nervous exhaustion, milling around like deranged gerbils. Surely working in an office would be easier than this. But then again, you wouldn't have to spend your Christmas with your family, so the ordeal may have been worth it. Unless, of course, you were stupid enough to bring them with you.

Have to say, though, that the airport looked a lot better on the inside than I'd expected, especially from this height. I could suddenly see why Brian Eno would make a whole album called *Music for Airports*, though listening to it I suspect he had an empty airport in mind, which is kind of a contradiction in terms. Needless to say, though, they weren't playing *Music for Airports* but Enya. Of course. Followed by The Corrs, followed by those bloody mammy's boys, Westlife. Thankfully you could hardly hear the tracks above the noise of thousands of people shouting at one another.

I finally stood in front of the vast screen with the departures information. The flight to New York was leaving, as scheduled, in an hour. I spent ten minutes hiding behind newspaper stands and potted plants, but I realised you'd need to be a special operative in the CIA to track someone down under these conditions, so I decided it would be a better plan to just buy a plane ticket and go directly to the terminal. That way I could make sure I was able to catch a glimpse of Lisa and Cecil, even if it cost eight hundred euros. Okay, a good look of him, though I did want to see Lisa too. For old time's sake and all that other stuff – namely jealousy and rejection.

When I finally got to the departure lounge, after more pushing and shoving, I casually made my way towards the seated area. I leant against the wall and pretended to read *The Celestine Prophecy* (which, incidentally, Lisa had given me before she left 'to help me cope', though I had no idea what she was talking about at the time). Anyway, I obviously wasn't making a very good job of it. I mean on either front. The coping or the going unnoticed in an airport full of people who looked capable of any form of violence. An air hostess kept looking over towards me, then began walking to where I was standing.

'Are you okay, sir?' she asked pointedly as she stood in front of me. I pretended to continue reading my book then looked up, after a moment, with surprise.

'You mean, me?'

'Yes.'

'Fine. Absolutely fine.'

'Are you taking flight EI105 to New York?' she asked, again in the same pointed tone.

'No. Not really,' I said, as calmly as possible.

'So…' she said, raising her perfectly plucked eyebrows into a perfectly formed arch.

'Just waiting to see a friend off. And her boyfriend.'

'I see.'

She walked away and I got the feeling that she thought I maybe had a bomb hidden in my bag or runners or even in that bloody book. I slid away and found a nice big potted palm tree to hide behind, with a good view of the desk and boarding area.

Just then, from my new vantage point, I saw Lisa walking towards a seat. I must say she looked a little frazzled, which I took as a good sign. Then I saw Cecil trailing behind her, dragging a massive case in one hand and a bunch of red roses in the other. I couldn't believe my eyes. The fuckin guy was wearing a poncho. *And* he was about fifty. I just couldn't understand how a woman of her intelligence would fall for that sentimental crap. I'd wooed her with some of the greatest lyrics ever written and she caved in the moment some dickhead in a blanket gave her flowers. Simply couldn't stand by and let her make such a fool of herself. The man was wearing a garment that hadn't been in fashion since 1968, for Christ sakes.

I leapt out from behind the palm tree and shouted out across the perfectly clean tiled floor that separated us: 'Lisa!'

She didn't seem to notice me for a second, but then her head turned slowly around to scan the crowd and finally found my expectant face.

'I love you. Come home. Please!' I shouted, so she could hear me above all the noise of people talking and the flight announcements. There were a lot of people gathering on the seat by now and they all suddenly stopped and turned to look at me. I guess maybe I'd said it louder than I realised. The air hostess had picked up a red phone but stood there absolutely still, staring at me with her mouth open.

'I've read the book. I get the point,' I continued. 'I'm a bit self-obsessed. I'll make it up to you, Honey, I promise,' I said, walking towards her, the sap in the poncho stepping back a couple of paces as if I was going to deck him or something.

Lisa turned round with one of her piercing looks. 'Tom, you're a total fuckwit, you know that? You really are,' she said, finally, in that hushed, angry voice I'd grown used to in the months we lived together. Call me naïve, but I hadn't expected her to be quite so hostile, given that the book she'd given me was all about forgiveness and life's great spiritual journey and all that bullshit.

She turned to poncho man. 'Tom, this is my fiancé, Rick. Rick – Tom. Tom – Rick.' She smiled momentarily. 'We're getting married in Manhattan in two weeks time. Now fuck off.'

Rick looked pretty scared, and I wondered if that last statement was meant for him and not me. The roses were on the floor in a pile.

'Rick, let's go,' Lisa said, and turned towards the air hostess who still had the phone in her hand. As poncho man gathered up the flowers Lisa stopped in her tracks, slowly turned round and stared at me, searching for an even more damning last insult. 'I can't believe you'd stoop so low. Not even you, Tom. Coming here like this to wreck my marriage plans. You're such a dink.'

I was in a state of total shock. In Lisa's repertoire of insults 'dink' was, for some reason, given special privilege and reserved only for people who didn't like her band's music. The silence lasted for approximately five seconds.

'He's here with me, darling,' a big, American voice boomed out.

We all turned. Jack of the green pants was standing beside me. He reached out his hand towards Lisa: 'Pleased to meet you. Jack O'Brien Snr. And you are?'

Even Lisa was stymied by that. 'Eh, Lisa… Evans… sir.'

'Tom here's been helping me set up a little business in Dublin. Music distribution. Country. All the rage these days.'

Lisa was gob-smacked and her face seemed to go through at least three emotions, which I couldn't quite unravel, before she said to me, 'So, you weren't here… for … I mean to…'

101

'Oh, eh, just a coincidence, Hon…. I didn't know you were getting married or anything,' I said, trying not to let the pain show through, but I guess it still did. Lisa now looked upset on my behalf.

'I'm *so* sorry Tom. It's just the way things happen.'

I stood there looking at that chessboard pattern of the tiled floor. Even Jack was quiet now.

'You've got to… let the happiness in Tom,' she said, as though she meant it.

'That's right, son,' said Jack, putting his giant arm about my shoulder. 'Let the happiness in. Exciting times ahead. Gotta move on. Just let it in. That's it.'

The air hostess broke the moment as she whispered into the microphone, 'All passengers for… one second… sorry… for Aer Lingus flight EL306… oh shit… sorry… for flight EI105 from Dublin to… John F Kennedy Airport, New York… now boarding.'

Everyone looked over as she sighed audibly into the microphone, then she forced a big *céad míle fáilte* Aer Lingus smile at the passengers who were staring at her. No one moved for a few seconds then everyone, including Lisa and poncho man, seemed to dash towards the desk.

I stood there with Jack, watching them all suddenly busy as they crowded round the air hostess, and found I really was speechless for the first time in my life.

'Son,' he said eventually, 'she's not your type. Trust me, I can tell these things.' And then he leaned close and said flatly, 'For heaven's sake she's marrying a man who wears a poncho, a garment that hasn't been worn in North America for nearly a century. At least not in New York city, apart from those stoned layabouts in Greenwich Village.'

'Thanks Jack,' I said, trying to keep my emotions under control. 'I think you might be right on that one.'

'You bet I am. Make no mistake about it. Trust me.'

He flashed that big smile again and I tried to smile back, but I'm sure it looked more like a grimace.

'Yeah, I suppose you're right.'

'Good. Now, I better get on that flight, son. Got a business to start, after all.'

He gathered his hand luggage and began to walk away, then turned. 'Great joke by the way, son. I'm going to use that on all my stationery. I can see already that you're going to be an asset to the company. I like your style. It takes guts to do what you just did there. Also like some of your ideas on bringing other types of music into the US. Got to be versatile. I'll give you a call after the festive season. Have a good one.'

Afterwards I sat on the bus as it moved slowly out of Dublin Airport. Lisa was right. I had to let it go, move on to new things. I rummaged in my bag and took out my iPod. I came across a new album Gary had given me. This was as good a start as any. I hit *Play*. I listened to a couple of tracks, not expecting to like it, but I had to admit it was pretty good. Keyboards were back. Big time. They called it electro-clash now (at least that's what Gary said) but I could see where they were coming from. It was good. Damn good. Best thing I'd heard in years, in fact. Moogs, fat synths, glitches and some smashing vocals. Boy that woman could sing. Lyrics: dynamite. I was beginning to feel better already and hardly noticed the houses we passed, or the cemetery, or the people on the bus. Just as the last track finished we crossed over the river and headed towards our final stop.

As I got off the bus and stepped onto D'Olier Street, I stopped for a moment to take off my headphones. As I put them in my bag a voice came from nowhere.

103

'Were you listening to Róisín Murphy?'

I turned round. A small, thin woman in her late twenties stood there in front of me, her black, dyed hair half covering her face.

'Yes,' I said, surprised.

'*Overpowered*?'

'Yeah. That's the one.'

'Great, isn't it?' she said as she pushed her hair away from her face, only for it to flop back down over it again.

'I like it. I only got it today but I really like it.'

'Yunno,' she said thoughtfully, 'really reminds me of all that early synth pop stuff, in a weird kind of way.'

Shit, I thought, is this a test? Is she just trying to call my bluff? Why did she say 'weird'? Was she trying to expose me? Out me? Ridicule me in front of all the tourists now getting off the bus; or even worse, in front of people who might actually know who Visage or Ultravox were?

'I love all that stuff as well. Depeche Mode. John Foxx...' she continued without the slightest hint of self-consciousness.

I couldn't contain myself. Anyone who even knew that John Foxx existed couldn't be a pretender. 'Japan,' I ventured, tentatively.

'Love Japan. Those fuckers from Duran Duran stole their fire big time. Totally ripped off *Quiet Life*. Anyway, they all moved on to better things and Duran Duran just got rich.'

Correct.

'And OMD. Strictly early period, though. Pre *Junk Culture*,' she ploughed on.

'Oh my God. Me too. *Architecture &...*'

'*Morality* is an absolute classic album,' we chimed.

Sweet Lord, she even used the word classic with the respect it deserved. I mean, beyond the vagaries of fashion

104

and taste and all that crap. We stood there in silence for a moment, amazed at each other.

'I'm Tom, by the way,' I said, losing the quiet game again, but I didn't mind this time.

'Me too,' she said.

'What?'

'Shit... I meant... Obviously, I'm not Tom... You're Tom. Jenny is what people call me,' she said, again pushing her hair aside, though this time leaving her hand there so it wouldn't fall back.

She was really pretty. Not like Lisa but in a different way. You know, quirky. She had this snubby nose and small, cute mouth. And it was certainly nice to hear my name spoken, you know, just as a name, for the third time in one day, and this time with maybe even a hint of curiosity instead of pity. Or, could it even be...

'What do *you* call you?' I asked her.

'Eh, Jenny, I suppose. So, what were you doing at the airport?'

'Nothing really. Just seeing a friend off kind of thing. You?'

'Just watching the planes taking off and landing,' she said off-handedly. 'Shit, can't believe you like all that old stuff. All coming back. Music is a circle. Everything comes back around eventually. Have you heard Plaid yet? Or Lali Puna? Or Boards of Canada?'

I liked her thesis. If country and western could make a comeback...

'No. Not yet. But I intend to,' I said with conviction. I already trusted her judgement.

'You've got to hear that stuff, Tom. Blow your socks off, I promise. I'll burn them for you.'

'That would be wonderful. Really, wonderful.'

We stood there awkwardly for a time, beside the buses as they came and went, or just idled beside us while the driver had a smoke; the illuminated point of the Spire rising up eerily behind the old buildings against the strange orange and smoky bronze of the sun, setting against the breaking clouds.

'So where you headed?' she asked eventually.

'Nowhere really. I mean anywhere, I guess. I don't know.'

'Me too. I mean…'

'Jenny,' I said, finally plucking up the courage, 'Do'ya wanna go for a coffee or something? If you have the time. You probably don't. I mean it doesn't have to be now or anything…'

'Yeah. No. Now's good.'

'Okay then. It's a date. Shit sorry… I didn't want to suggest…'

'Bewley's?'

'Sounds great,' I said, breathlessly.

We started walking up the street towards Trinity College.

'So Jenny, what da'ya do with yourself?' *Stupid question. Too obvious.*

'You know. Stuff. I was just working on a remix on the bus,' she said casually.

I have to admit the idea that she was a musician had caught me off-guard. In my limited experience, musicians are different to your standard music lover like me. They actually have a purpose in life.

'Yeah. I was working on a remix of Gary Numan's "Cars".'

'Right.'

'Would you be so kind?'

'What?' I asked, surprised.

'Bassline please, maestro.'

Wasn't sure what she meant, so I just started singing the baseline with gusto like I'd done that time in Platinum Discs all those years before. DO DI-DU, DO DI-DU, DU-DI-DOO… Exactly on cue, Jenny came in with the vocal line:

'Here on my bus / I feel safest of all / I can lock all my doors / It's the on-ly way to live.' DO DI-DU 'On bus-*es*.' DU-DI-DO…

'Here on my bus / I can only receive / I can listen to you / It keeps me stable for nights…' DO DI-DU 'On bus-*es*.' DU-DI-DO, DO-DO-DO-DO-DOOO…

'Next verse. You sing it, I'm on instruments.'

'Here on my bus,' I croaked, 'Where the image breaks down / Will you vis-it me please? / If I open my door… on bus-*es*…' DUM DI DUM, DO-DI-DO…

For the second time on the same day, I found I had a crowd of people looking at me with the same mixture of bafflement, amusement and, I guess, pity. I was getting used to it, and Jenny didn't seem to mind either. It was 4.37. I know, because I looked up at the Trinity clock to be sure, then back at Jenny, this time starting out on the fourth verse together, ignoring everyone around us.

'Here in my bus / I know I've started to think / About leaving tonight / Although nothing seems right / On bus-*es*… DO DI-DU, DU-DI-DO, DO DI-DU, DU-DI-DO, DO DI-DU, DU-DI-DO, DO-DO-DO-DO-DOOO.'

Jenny and I beamed at each other. To my surprise there was a round of applause from what looked like a coach-full of middle-aged, American tourists who had gathered round us. Maybe I was onto something. The Americans would love this stuff and maybe that stuff Jenny had mentioned as well. Jack was right too. You have to diversify. The future was looking bright even as the darkness descended over Trinity and the occasional seagull circled overhead. Yes, indeed. Big time as Gary is fond of saying when something good is happening.

Or was about to.

# Acknowledgements

I would like to offer my sincere gratitude to the following: Dr Adrian Frazier, Department of English, National University of Ireland, Galway; Mark Carter, Greg O'Brien and Richard Lubell, for their eagle-eyed observations on the manuscript; Bernice Mulligan for her advice on German; Niall MacMonagle for his constant support and generosity; Adele Ward for her sharp reading and editing of the two pieces included, and Mike Fortune-Wood for his cover design and backroom work; and, finally, to Adele and Mike, the Ward and the Wood, for seeing fit to publish this book. My sincere thanks to all.

I would also like to express my gratitude to, and admiration for, all of the bands and artists cited or quoted in this book